It's just a dream . . .

But was it? Everything seemed so real to Hillary . . . too real. The old de Gaetano house stood below her, nestled in the family vineyards. But she'd never seen that house! Not even in pictures! It had never stood in her lifetime.

"Is anybody here?" The frantic tone of her own voice startled her. She seemed to be the only person in the world. "Jeff, can you hear me?" Why wasn't her friend answering her?

"Help me!" she called. "Jeff, help me wake up!"

There was no comforting touch of her friend's hand on her shoulder, but she could feel a presence. The sky was darkening and something evil was approaching beneath the midnight veil of clouds. Hillary didn't dare turn for fear she'd see her own death approaching.

I must wake up! "Please," she whispered.

Behind her came the thundering sound of hoofbeats.

Dear Reader,

When I was given the enthusiastic go-ahead to complete *Dangerous Vintage* for Intrigue, I was extremely excited. I was also somewhat surprised, since this story—with its wayward ghost—is more than a bit unusual.

I'd long meant to write a story set in the Napa Valley. The area, with its tradition of wine-making, conjured sensual images of lovers meeting beneath grape arbors, joyful wine toasts, and merry reverie. I'd also wanted to write a good old-fashioned ghost story, but one that worked as a regular mystery, too. The result, I'm happy to say, is *Dangerous Vintage*—a book that Harlequin found so unusual and so compelling that they named it a "Dreamscape" title. It's a ghost story and a murder mystery combined, with lots of romance between two old friends who have always hoped to mean even more to each other.

I thought imagining and creating a ghost might be fun . . . and it was! I truly hope you'll enjoy the unusual elements in this story every bit as much as I have.

Very best wishes,

Laura Pender

Dangerous Vintage

Laura Pender

Harlequin Books

TORONTO • NEW YORK • LONDON
AMSTERDAM • PARIS • SYDNEY • HAMBURG
STOCKHOLM • ATHENS • TOKYO • MILAN
MADRID • WARSAW • BUDAPEST • AUCKLAND

The smack of California earth shall
linger on the palate of your grandson.
—Robert Louis Stevenson

Harlequin Intrigue edition published January 1993

ISBN 0-373-22212-2

DANGEROUS VINTAGE

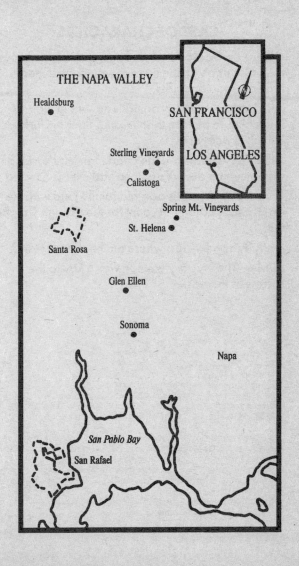

THE NAPA VALLEY

Healdsburg

Sterling Vineyards

Calistoga

Spring Mt. Vineyards

St. Helena

Glen Ellen

Sonoma

Napa

Santa Rosa

San Pablo Bay

San Rafael

SAN FRANCISCO

LOS ANGELES

CAST OF CHARACTERS

Hillary de Gaetano—As a winegrower, she knew that this year's grape harvest would yield more than the regular spirits.

Jeff Simpson—The pragmatic newsman was beginning to believe that unusual dangers lurked in Hillary's vineyards.

Albert de Gaetano—The dead man left shocking evidence of a dual life no one had ever suspected.

Bernard Foche—His age-old family feud with the de Gaetanos didn't account for the strange way he felt.

Emily Pragger—Just where did her loyalties lie?

Marie—The mystery woman was a key to the secrets of the past.

Prologue

The man stood on the low hill with his back to her, the skirt of his black coat fluttering in the wind like the wings of a large bird. Beyond him the vineyards and the winery lay seemingly deserted. Wrongly deserted, Hillary thought, for it was full day and the vines were heavy with fruit.

"What is this?" she asked him.

He shook his head but didn't reply.

"Tell me!" She grasped his arm, turning him.

"It's all gone, Marie. All gone," he said in a mournful whisper. And, before Hillary had time to really see his face, it dissolved, flowing off his skull like thin putty, the bones beneath it crumbling to dust.

And then she was alone on the hill overlooking the now-withered vines and decaying buildings of her family vineyard. Alone forever.

Chapter One

It was only a dream.

Hillary de Gaetano didn't believe in omens or other fortune-telling rubbish. She wouldn't be as successful as she was if she allowed for any possibility of such things being true. Since she'd taken over the financial end of de Gaetano Enterprises, the family's business holdings and stock portfolio had run against the trends to become more profitable and efficient. She'd managed that through hard work and concentration, not foolish superstition.

So it was hard for Hillary to admit that the dream had gotten to her. It was harder still for her to act on the impulse it provoked. But she had acted, and now she was on a flight from New York to the Napa Valley following the illogical feelings that had grown from that dream.

If it had only been the dream, she would have forgotten about it easily. But since that night when she had awakened, shivering in her midtown Manhattan apartment, it was as though there was always someone beside her whispering dire warnings about her home and family. Sometimes, when the office was quiet, she could swear she had heard his voice again. "Gone," he said. "Hurry."

Finally, she'd decided to call her cousin, Albert, who managed the vineyards. Maybe if she heard him tell her that everything was all right, she would quit this needless worrying. Maybe.

Of course Albert had assured her that the de Gaetano vineyards and winery were moving toward harvest without a hitch. "All systems go," he'd said, laughing over the phone. But his words didn't ring true to her practiced ear. She'd heard the same note of misgiving in the voices of executives whose businesses hadn't earned what had been projected. She knew when someone was covering up something.

Albert and Hillary de Gaetano had been left as the sole owners of both the de Gaetano winery and de Gaetano Enterprises, two very different businesses that had been built over the years by the family. As the last family members in a family business, Albert and Hillary had split the management of the holdings between them, Hillary going to New York and Albert remaining with the winery. They worked well together, and the businesses had done well under them primarily because of their closeness and their easy communication. But because they were family, there was also a desire to protect each other that might cause Albert to hedge a bit on bad news. And it might be that what he wasn't telling her was worse than he thought.

Her apprehension had grown over the week since that call, until it had become a constant sense of dread. Finally, she'd given into the growing uneasiness and booked the flight home to the Napa Valley. Something was wrong. She could feel it. And, though she couldn't explain it, she knew she'd have to go in person to alleviate her apprehension.

Now, instead of feeling relieved to be out of the city and on her way back to the quiet familiarity of the valley, Hillary felt increasingly uneasy as she approached her destination. She couldn't help feeling that everything was going horribly wrong somehow and she was too late to prevent it.

JEFF SIMPSON REGARDED the copy on the video screen before him with disinterest. He'd been at odds with himself the past couple days and couldn't keep his mind on his duties as the publishing editor of *The Napa Press*. It was as if there was a faint smell of smoke in the air, and he occasionally caught a whiff that caused him to ponder what might be burning. But there was no real smell and nothing else was out of the ordinary. Still, he had an unsettled feeling.

The Napa Press, the small weekly paper Jeff's family had founded, would be going to press tonight. The compact office was buzzing with as much activity as the five-person staff could muster, while Jeff tried to recapture the line of thought he'd been pursuing for this week's editorial. It was no use. The redistricting plan for California wine-growing regions didn't seem important any longer.

What he was principally interested in was Albert de Gaetano and his strange behavior the past couple weeks. The normally effusive young man had become brusque on the street and had spent an unusual amount of time in San Francisco lately. It wasn't like him. But it wasn't Jeff's place to nose into de Gaetano business. Unless there was a story in it, of course.

Smiling, Jeff walked to his office to use the phone. Maybe Hillary could enlighten him on the matter. If nothing else, it was a good excuse to call her in New York. Hearing that wonderful voice again might break his lousy mood.

BY THE TIME JEFF CALLED her office, Hillary had landed in San Francisco and had retrieved her Mercedes from the long-term lot. Before leaving for home, she called Albert. There was no answer at the winery office or at his house, and the lack of response served to increase her sense of urgency. She had to get home.

As she made her way north through the rush-hour traffic, she began to relax. The feeling of foreboding that had brought her across the continent was fading.

That's better, she thought. *You just needed a break. That's all. There never was anything wrong except that you needed to get home and put your feet up for a couple days. Now that you're here, you might as well do just that.*

When she rounded San Pablo Bay and began driving north into the Napa Valley, she was smiling. It was just as peaceful as she'd expected it to be. In less than an hour she'd be in her own house with no worries other than to hope there were still some canned goods available for dinner. Maybe this trip was necessary, after all.

THE STRAWBERRY-ORANGE glow of the sun just touched the Mayacamas Mountains beyond the family vineyards surrounding her home near the town of St. Helena in the Napa Valley. Hillary sat and sipped a cup of hot herbal tea and tried to think of someone she could call. The field foreman at the vineyard had assured her that the vines were healthy and ripening well, but he was no help in locating Albert. "Might be in San Francisco," he'd suggested, but he hadn't seen him at all that day.

Emily Pragger, Albert's assistant, didn't know of any travel plans, but then she didn't always know in advance these days. According to her, Albert had cut back on his work schedule lately, and had taken to traveling into the city more often than usual. Still, Emily hadn't sounded worried when Hillary talked to her. And, if not for her own sense of foreboding, Hillary wouldn't have been worried, either.

It appeared that she could do little but wait until morning to talk to her cousin. Wait and watch the sunset alone.

Waiting wasn't Hillary's strong suit.

She thought of calling Jeff Simpson, the publisher of the local weekly newspaper and her closest friend in town, but he would be busy tonight. It was Tuesday, the night they put *The Napa Press* together for publication. Because it was mid-summer, most of her other friends were away and those available were tied to family chores at this time of day. There was no one who might welcome a conversation. Feeling lonely, it suddenly seemed unfortunate that she wasn't married at thirty-two.

But then it wasn't her routine to be in California at this time of year. Her duties were in New York. Though the family business, first and foremost, had been winemaking, they had diversified throughout the seventies, to help provide a solid base of income that would see them through the vagaries of weather and public taste that affected the wine business.

The breeze through the valley was picking up, ruffling the leaves of the grapevines that stretched beyond her window and to the faraway mountains. Albert must have left a window open somewhere in the house when he'd checked on it while she was in New York. She felt a tendril of the wind flutter past the back of her neck like a hand lovingly tracing a line across her shoulders.

Putting her teacup aside on the glass table in the solarium adjoining the living room, she stood and stretched her lean body slowly, working her hands up through her long, sandy-blond hair. Then she prowled back into the nearly dark house.

Her teacup rattled on the table behind her. Hillary turned, walking back until she could see it on the table. She couldn't tell if it had moved or not. Perhaps there'd been a slight tremor that she hadn't noticed because she'd been walking.

A brief scuffling sound surprised her as she stepped back inside the living room. It sounded like someone walking with a furtive sliding step, and she almost called out to ask who was in the house. Then she stopped herself and walked toward the kitchen, shaking her head and smiling.

But she heard the sound again, closer this time. Hillary turned quickly, scanning the floor for an explanation of the sound. She froze as a strange shivering feeling raised the hair on the back of her neck. It felt for a moment as though a man had placed his hand on her shoulder, and then she heard it. A voice, whispering so quietly that she felt certain she'd imagined it, yet it spoke with such insistence that it startled her.

"Fire," it said. And then her strange chill was gone with the voice, replaced by the certainty that she should listen to the warning. Whether it was simple intuition or a warning from beyond, she wasn't about to equivocate. Initially, she'd come to the valley on her intuition of disaster, and this current feeling was more intense than the one she'd followed across the continent. She had to get to the winery fast.

Hillary drove her Mercedes convertible as fast as possible along the narrow road from the house to the winery. She had to get there fast or it would be too late. *All gone.* Was this what her dream had been about? There was no time to think of anything but keeping the car on the road as she rushed through the twilight fields.

Everything seemed normal when she skidded to a halt before the mission-style buildings housing the presses and the vats used for crushing and fermenting the grapes. But she could see a faint orange glow through a side window. She fumbled with her keys at the door. When she finally burst in, she saw the glow of fire inside the winery office!

There was a fire extinguisher on a rack just inside. She grabbed the heavy bottle and directed the jet of carbon dioxide through the door to the inner office. She took a deep breath and stepped toward the fire.

The flames were confined to the far wall. They climbed from behind the desk and file cabinets, licked at the curtains and tried to find purchase in the flame-retardant ceiling tiles. Hillary extinguished the curtains quickly, and then quenched the flames that had reached the papers stacked beside the computer console on the desk.

With the fire out, the room was thrown into darkness, but she didn't dare switch on the lights until she knew more about the source of the fire. There was a large flashlight in the extinguisher rack. She brought it in and moved the beam of light around the room. Now she could see smoke coming from the drawers of a file cabinet. Keeping her hand away from the scorching-hot metal, she rolled a large manila envelope into a tight tube and used it to pull open the drawers and spray the contents with icy blasts of gas. At last, the fire was out.

Hillary dropped the heavy extinguisher, wiping her brow. It had been a close call. If she hadn't been warned when she was, they might have lost everything.

Warned? How?

No, don't think about that now. The fire should be her only concern at the moment, but it was hard to push her questions from her mind. Where had the eerie voice originated from?

By sliding one of the file cabinets forward slightly, she could see that the flames had apparently started in an electrical outlet behind it. It must have gotten hot and ignited the rolled blueprints and survey maps that her cousin usually slipped back above the wide oak baseboard for storage. Following the cord from the receptacle, she found that the computer on the desk was plugged in there. Sure enough, though the screen was blank now, the switch was in the on position. Either Albert or Emily had forgotten to turn it off.

Well, that was simple enough. For good measure, she doused the plug with gas, and then she went to find the circuit box and turned off the electricity. The walls were stone, so there wasn't much danger of fire lurking within them, but she'd sooner be safe than sorry, at least until the fire department could investigate further.

She was about to dial when she paused to look up at the center of the ceiling. Three fire sprinkler nozzles hung down like daisy petals in a row. Why hadn't they started? They were supposed to be activated by heat, and the flame had licked over the nearest one. They should have flooded the fire before she had even arrived, but all they'd managed was a feeble dribble of water.

Why hadn't they been activated?

Hillary hung up the phone and ran back to the work area where the pipes running forward to the offices split from the main lines. There was her answer.

The sprinklers had been shut off at the source!

"IT HADN'T BEEN BURNING long. You put it all out with the extinguisher." Chief Ned Jagger of the St. Helena fire department slapped his uniform hat lightly against his left leg as he stood with Hillary before the winery building. "The building is stone, and the wiring was all added on top of the walls, so there isn't much danger of missing any embers."

"So we're safe and sound?" Hillary regarded the older man thoughtfully, wondering how to broach the subject of the sprinkler system.

"Oh, yes, perfectly safe. Just have an electrician fix the wiring and have it inspected before turning the juice back on." He glanced back at the building and frowned slightly. "I don't know if your insurance company will be very happy about it, though."

"Why?"

"Because of that sprinkler system being off like that," he said. "I imagine someone fixed a leak or something and forgot to turn it back on. But because they messed up, you'll likely be paying the damages out of your own pocket.''

"I suppose so," she admitted. "But then, if it had been on, the damage from the water may well have been worse than the fire."

"Probably," he said, putting on his hat. "I wonder about something else, though. The file cabinets shouldn't have burned inside like that. Not that badly, anyway."

"What do you mean?" She hadn't given the cabinets much thought. "They aren't fireproof."

"No, but they weren't wide open, either, not until you pulled them open. There wouldn't normally have been enough air available inside to get such a good fire going. And there are no openings in the back that could have let the flames in to begin with."

"Meaning, what?"

"I don't know. In some circumstances, it would look like the fire was deliberate. But since you're the one who put out the fire, I probably wouldn't go that far."

"What if I had just made certain the files were burned, and then put it out to save the rest of the office?"

"No, that would have looked suspicious," he said. "And that's another reason I don't see this one as arson. It's probably just a strange fluke."

"Yes, I suppose an arsonist would have let most of the office burn so it wouldn't look suspicious, and then turned on the sprinklers to maintain a look of normalcy."

"If he were smart, he would."

"It's something to think about, anyway."

"Yes, it is at that. We'll be going now. You take care."

"Yes, and thank you for coming so quickly."

Hillary watched the yellow truck drive away, but her thoughts were back in the smoke-damaged office. Had the fire been deliberately set? Why? Maybe, if Albert would get back from wherever he had gone, she could get an answer.

There were no answers at the winery, so Hillary took her questions home alone. But the questions wouldn't go away. Why would anyone want to burn the files at the winery? Who might be incriminated by anything in the files other than an employee? Anything in those files would already be common knowledge to Albert and Emily Pragger, so nothing could be hidden by burning them. Unless Albert . . . no, that was absurd. He certainly hadn't set the fire.

Hillary called her cousin as soon as she got home. The telephone was busy, which was certainly a good sign. If she still couldn't talk to him, at least she knew he was home again. Now his unavailability angered her. If he was in town, the least he could do is answer his phone.

When she called his number again, there was no response. Where had he gone now, and why? As if answering her question, her telephone rang almost as soon as she'd hung up.

She scooped up the receiver eagerly. "Hello? Albert?"

"Hi, stranger, it's Jeff. Sorry to disappoint you."

"I'm not disappointed," she said, laughing. "I thought of calling you earlier but I knew you'd be busy. I didn't want to disturb you."

"So you gave us a fire instead." He laughed, and Hillary could imagine the teasing twinkle in her friend's happy blue eyes. "We'll have to rearrange the paper a bit to fit in the story."

"I probably should have held the fire until after deadline," she said. "How'd you hear about it?"

"Police scanner. Since it was out already, I didn't bother sending anyone with a camera. Are you all right?"

"I'm fine, and the damage was superficial."

"Good. What happened?"

"Faulty wiring," she said. "A plug got hot and some papers caught fire."

"Are you sure it was accidental?" he asked quickly, but with a reporter's detached air.

"As sure as I can be. Why?" What was he leading up to?

"I spoke to Ned, and he said that...well, he as much as said that he thinks someone may have set the fire," Jeff answered flatly.

"But—" Hillary cut off her disavowal. "He didn't seem so convinced when we spoke, but it did come up. Is this an official interview? On the record?"

"Kind of, I guess. But I don't have space in the paper for a big story, so I won't be doing any speculating."

"Good." Hillary was doing her own speculating, and arson was beginning to seem more likely. The sprinklers were off and that was too convenient. The burned papers in the cabinets were too hard to explain.

"Why did you go to the winery at all? Couldn't you let work go for one night?" There was laughter in his hearty baritone. He knew her work habits quite well.

"I had a feeling," she said slowly. "A premonition, I guess, that something was wrong."

"That'll be a good headline," he said. "Premonition Saves Winery."

"You wouldn't want to make me look like a fool, would you?"

"No, guess not. What's Albert got to say about the fire?"

"I haven't been able to reach him yet," she said.

"I'll give him a call," Jeff said. "Can I buy you lunch tomorrow?"

"Sure. I'll stop by the paper."

"Sounds good. Bye."

He hung up, leaving her thinking about Albert again. It was after eleven o'clock now, far later than he would usually go out. Where had he gone? She dialed his number one more time, but no one answered. He had to be there, so it seemed that the only way she'd be able to contact him was to go in person.

HILLARY CROSSED the Napa River into the small community of St. Helena twenty minutes later. She skirted the downtown area and headed toward Albert's house. A confirmed bachelor, Albert nonetheless shared the wine lover's enjoyment of company, and so he'd purchased the large house after declining Hillary's offer of her smaller, more secluded house in the vineyards.

After finding that Albert's car was in the garage, Hillary approached the front door feeling somewhat unsure of herself. At first she'd been angry at his absence, but now she felt almost afraid. What if something had happened to him? She rang the bell.

There was no response. She was about to try the knob when the sound of a car turning into the drive stopped her. It was Jeff's dusty Jeep. It came to a halt behind her Mercedes.

"Not answering his phone?" Jeff jumped out and joined her on the step. He quickly kissed her cheek as he clasped her hand. "Welcome home," he said. Light seemed to gleam in his eyes.

"Thank you. But I guess you didn't come here to talk to me."

"No, I wanted something from Al about the fire for the story. We've got to go to press in a couple hours. I didn't get any answer on the phone."

"Me neither, but I know he's home. At least, I do now. His car is in the garage."

"Maybe he's asleep. Or he might have walked somewhere."

"He's not that sound a sleeper." Hillary tried the knob, and the door opened. "And he wouldn't have left the house unlocked if he had gone anywhere." Pushing the door, she stepped across the threshold. "Albert?"

"Al?" Jeff joined her in the front hall, his hand protectively on her shoulder.

"I'll check upstairs," she said. "Check down here, okay?"

"Sure thing, Hill."

Hillary climbed the stairs that rose beside the entrance hall opposite the living room. There was a strange, bitter smell in the air that she couldn't quite place, though it was familiar. Upstairs she looked into his bedroom first. The bed was made and everything seemed in order. The same was true of the guest room. But outside the closed door of the third bedroom, which Albert used as his home office, the smell she'd noticed was unavoidable. Wine. It was the bitter smell of stale wine. The alcohol had evaporated, leaving only the scents of acids and fruit sugars.

But the smell didn't warn her of anything amiss. Even in this quantity, it was too common an odor to her. It didn't seem alarming. She opened the door to the office and stepped in, her foot crunching on broken glass in the carpeting.

A wine bottle lay shattered by an unbroken companion. Had Albert had intruders? The desk before her was empty except for a third bottle. It was on its side, lying in a pool of fragrant wine, next to the telephone. Turning toward a couch that was partly hidden by the open door, Hillary saw him.

"My God!" Her voice failed her as she looked at his bloodied face and at the blood on the couch.

"Jeff! God, hurry!" She was able to scream the words at last. She stood transfixed. Albert's blood had been spilled as freely as the wine from the bottles, and it was as dark as the boldest vintage. Only when Jeff rushed into the room was she able to move, throwing herself into his arms and giving in to the tortured sobbing that had claimed her heart.

Chapter Two

It's all gone.

When the man spoke this time, there was clear evidence of his meaning. The winery in the valley below them was burned to the ground, the vines trampled and dead beneath a sun that seemed to swell in omnipotent mastery overhead.

No, you're wrong. I stopped the fire. I put it out.

In her dream, Hillary's voice was thick and slow, the intensity of her protest dulled to an urgent murmur by lazy intonation. She had put the fire out. She remembered that. The devastation before them was a lie.

Everything is all right now, she said. *Go tell Albert that everything is all right.*

All gone, he repeated. Then he turned toward her, fixing his mournful stare on Hillary as they stood on the hill, the dry wind snapping his coattails and whipping her hair against her eyes.

Jeff? Indeed, it seemed to be Jeff's face beneath the formal, black, western-style hat, though his visage was distorted, broadened and harshened as though he'd suffered through the same cataclysm that had burned the winery.

It's hopeless. He shook his head, horrible sadness showing in his eyes. *Love is hopeless.*

Tell Albert, she said, urgently. *Tell Albert.*

But he was gone, and the valley was gone with him. *Tell Albert.*

"TELL ALBERT."

Hillary heard her own voice in the still air of her bedroom when she woke. Yes, she thought, she'd have to tell Albert. But tell him what?

No, she wouldn't be telling him anything. Albert was dead.

Suddenly, she was fully awake and standing beside the bed. The dim light of day crept past the drawn shades. A ragged gasp of sudden despair forced itself up from the pit of her stomach, shaking her whole body with the force of her grief. He was dead.

Dead! Her cousin had been brutally murdered, and the bleak dream of the burned winery suddenly seemed pleasant in comparison to the fact with which she had to live. Albert had been murdered, and she felt like a coward for having given in to the shelter of sleep. She ran her hands over her rumpled jeans and blouse, trying to remember how she'd gotten to bed or when. All she could remember just then was the sight of Albert's body and the sound of someone saying, "All gone."

Some of that was a dream, wasn't it? Yes, someone had been talking in the dream, but she wasn't sure who it had been or what else they may have said. She was all twisted around and adrift on a riptide of emotions. Her flight, the fire and Albert's death were muddled together in her mind and tied up with images of destruction in the dream. What was gone? Albert was gone.

He's really dead!

Choking back a sob, Hillary rushed out of her bedroom to the sun-bright living room hoping to find something to repudiate her memories. There was still a chance that she was wrong, wasn't there? She'd dreamed that he was dead. That was it, wasn't it? Couldn't that be the explanation? Please? Everything in the house was just as tidy as it had been when she arrived. What had happened?

"Hillary?"

Startled, she spun toward the voice behind her. Jeff was sitting on the couch by the window stifling a yawn with one hand. His hair was rumpled, but he didn't look as though he'd been sleeping. And, judging by the dark hollows encasing his worried eyes, it didn't appear that he'd slept all night. "Are you all right?" he asked, rising.

It had to be true. Albert was dead! There was no escaping that reality.

"I don't know. I—" The sorrow within her threatened to overwhelm her just then; tears strained to fall from her eyes. But she held them in check with a deep, shuddering breath. "Oh, God, Jeff," she said softly. "What happened?"

"We don't know for sure." Jeff gathered her into his arms and held her tightly to him. He had no idea what to tell her, but he desperately wanted to make it right somehow. Hillary's happiness was all that mattered to him, and he'd do anything to maintain that happiness. Unfortunately, there was no way to cushion the blow now, no way to make things right.

"We just don't know what happened, honey," he said, feeling absolutely worthless to her. "There hasn't been time to sort it all out yet."

"But he was shot," Hillary said, clinging to Jeff as she remembered last night's events. "Did someone break in? Was there a struggle? I don't understand."

"I don't, either," Jeff conceded. "There was no sign of a struggle. Or that anyone else had been there, for that matter. Don't worry, we'll get to the bottom of this."

"Who would want to harm him? Who?"

She voiced her answerless question in a halting tone of hopelessness, a sound so foreign to her voice that Jeff felt his heart breaking at the loneliness in it. "We'll get him." That was all he could say in response to that terribly anguished sound. "We'll make him pay."

"If we can find him," Hillary said, regaining her composure. She wasn't the type of woman to give in to tragedy. There must be something she could do now, if only to maintain her sanity. "What did the police say? Were there any clues?"

Hillary drew back to look at Jeff, her cheeks moist with sorrow. She hadn't been in the room for the preliminary investigation, so she hadn't spoken to the policemen or seen the evidence at hand. Now Jeff was reluctant to talk about it, though he knew they'd have to discuss it. All he wanted to do was hold her safely to him a moment longer.

"There didn't appear to be anything helpful in the room," he said. "The police are hoping that Albert might have mentioned any problems to a friend who could give them a lead. Had you spoken to him lately? Did he say anything to you?"

"No, not to me." Hillary snuggled back into his arms briefly, enjoying the comfort afforded by her old friend's nearness. "I called last week," she said, breaking away at last. "He said that everything was running smoothly. Why?"

"He seemed a bit distracted to me lately, is all."

"Distracted?" Hillary didn't dare bring up her own distractions over the past few weeks, fearing she'd appear a fool, but what if Albert had shared those feelings? What if it was knowledge of his impending death that was lurking at the edge of her thoughts rather than some vaguely ominous feelings about the winery.

"Just an impression, really." Jeff regarded her closely, noting the thoughtful expression that pushed worry from her eyes. She'd be all right. He knew that look and knew the woman who wore it well enough to know that she would weather the storm. "And I don't suppose it had anything to do with this."

"No, probably not. What a hopeless mess." Hillary walked slowly to the kitchen, her mouth suddenly dry. If she could concentrate on things as carefully as possible, she could hold on to her composure. Only in that way would she be able to avoid falling into despair. She tried to straighten her clothing as she walked, noticing that the snap of her jeans had been undone. "Who put me to bed last night? I don't remember a thing."

"I did." Jeff walked into the kitchen behind her, leaning against the stove. "You fell asleep in the car, and I didn't have the heart to wake you. I hope you don't mind."

"Not at all." She snapped her jeans shut, thinking of how her father had put her to bed countless times when she'd fallen asleep at her homework or in front of the television as a child. The burly man would carry her gently to her room, pull off her shoes and unsnap her jeans for comfort, and leave her with a kiss on the forehead that was always remembered on waking. The thought brought a new sense of loss to her mind, but a pleasantly familiar one this time. "You carried me all the way in from the car?" she asked, forcing herself to speak of mundane things.

"Don't worry." Jeff laughed. "It wasn't any great strain."

"Thank you." She couldn't believe her good fortune in having a friend such as Jeff. So steady and true, he was her perfect port in any storm, the one person she could depend upon for any manner of aid or comfort.

"I'd do anything for you, Hillary." He patted her arm lightly as she ran the tap to fill a glass with cold water.

"I know," she admitted, thinking of the long and sturdy friendship that preceded those words. She knew that he wasn't just mouthing pleasant consolation but stating a heartfelt fact that went to the core of their friendship.

"You didn't have to stay," she said.

"I wanted to be handy. How do you feel?"

"Not bad, physically." The water tasted bitter, as though nothing would ever taste right again. "I feel a bit numb otherwise, though. Last night is a blur to me. All I remember is finding Albert and sitting with a policeman in the kitchen to give him my statement. I don't even remember what I told him."

"You were in shock. That's about all that did happen, though. Mostly, we were in the officers' way."

"So, what happened?"

"He was shot." Jeff stepped out to the dining room, unsure of how much description he should divulge. If she couldn't remember, then he'd rather that she didn't try. His own memory of the horrible sight in Albert's study was too much for him to take. He'd rather that the details remained a blur to her.

"I know that," Hillary said, following with her glass and sitting at the dining room table. "But how and why? Who would have done it?"

"The front door was open," Jeff offered. "It could have been anyone."

"Nobody would want to kill Albert. Not even Bernie Foche would go that far," she said, naming a neighboring grower with long-standing enmity for her family. "I don't believe any of it."

"Hillary." Jeff pulled out the chair beside her, sitting carefully. "There was one strange thing about it that I probably should mention to you now before you hear it somewhere else. The police noticed it, but I don't know if it meant anything or not."

"Yes, Jeff?" Noting the anxious look in her friend's eyes, Hillary braced herself for shocking news. Anything that Jeff Simpson was reluctant to tell her must be bad news, indeed.

"Albert was shot in the mouth," he said, stopping himself when he saw her shuddering reaction. The image conjured up by such simple words was thoroughly distasteful to him, and he didn't want to say it any more than she wanted to hear it.

"Go on," Hillary said. She still couldn't reconcile that to her vague memories of the night. All she remembered was blood and her cousin's startled eyes staring at her. She forced the memory of what she'd seen in her cousin's office from her mind, lest it consume her with grief. She had to be strong now, and ready to hear what Jeff had to say so that she could begin to make some sense of it.

"Well, the police noticed that the angle of the wound and the fact that there was blood on his right hand seemed to point toward . . . well, suicide."

"Suicide! No!" She hadn't expected something like that. Albert? Never.

"But everything about the way he was found makes it look that way except that—" Jeff grasped her hand "—there was no gun in the room. No weapon."

"Then it wasn't suicide," Hillary said, relieved.

"No, it couldn't be," he assured her. "The police said it might have been, but that someone might have come later and removed the gun."

"That's absurd! Why would anyone take the gun?"

He shrugged. "It was only a spur of the moment theory, Hillary. I only told you now so you would be prepared if the police mentioned it to you." He continued watching her with worried eyes, happy to see the resolve in her features. "Someone may have wanted it to look like murder."

"Thank you for telling me. But I'd imagine that the police have dropped that idea already." She spoke with growing conviction. "After all, there would be no reason to want a suicide to appear to be murder, though the murderer might have wanted it to look like suicide."

"That seems most likely." But Jeff couldn't for the life of him figure out why the murderer would take the gun away after creating such a convincing suicide. Such doubts had no place in their conversation today, and he smiled to cover them. There would be time for doubts and questions later. Now his task was to provide comfort. "I'm really sorry, Hillary."

"Thank you, Jeff," she said. "I'd be lost right now without you."

"No, you'd be just fine."

They regarded each other fondly for a moment, taking solace in the history they had in common. They'd grown up together and had shared so much over the years that a glance was often enough to communicate all that needed to be said. Hillary knew that Jeff would take on her burden for her if he could, and she knew that her feelings were mirrored in his. Albert's death affected him all the more because it had such a large impact on her. For his sake, she'd have to be strong. He didn't deserve to carry her burden no matter how much he might want to shoulder it.

"I'm all right now," she assured him, squeezing his hand. "You don't have to worry about me."

"Hillary I—" Jeff stopped, a rueful smile gracing his broad expressive lips. "What brought you back to town?" he asked, simply.

"I just wanted to come back," she said. What had he begun to say? She couldn't tell from his concerned expression.

"Hell of a vacation you're having."

"It wasn't really a vacation." She thought about her reasons for returning home and wondered if they'd make any sense to Jeff. She'd thought they were foolish once, but now she wasn't so sure. Her general feelings of foreboding had certainly taken on a specific form, hadn't they?

"Back on business, then?"

"No, I came back on a hunch, really." It was obvious she'd have to tell him something. He was only making small talk, trying to provide a semblance of normalcy for her, but if she seemed to be evading an answer, he'd worry that something else was troubling her. Besides, even if he laughed—which she couldn't imagine him doing—his opinion had always been valuable to her. She needed it more than ever in this situation. "I had a feeling that something was wrong. Nothing specific, but definitely a feeling that something bad was going to happen. That's why I came back."

"A feeling?" Jeff's brows knit with thought as he looked at her, his sturdy jaw tightening. "Are you sure Albert didn't say something?"

"No," she admitted. "I have no logical reason for it. I just had a feeling. You know? A feeling like something was wrong and I should get back here as soon as possible. Unfortunately, I didn't get here fast enough."

"It's hardly your fault, Hill—" Jeff began.

"I know." She cut him off with a sorrowful sigh. "But I should have stopped trying to be logical and gone with my feelings. I'd have been here a week earlier if I had."

"Which doesn't mean that Albert would have told you anything, even if he knew he was in trouble." Jeff spoke with the conviction of a man determined to shelter her from her own sense of duty and guilt. "He could have called you anytime he wanted to talk about it."

"You almost sound as though you believe it might be suicide."

"No way," he said adamantly. "But something was bothering him. He'd spent a considerable amount of time drinking last night."

"Albert didn't drink to excess."

"No, he didn't," Jeff said pointedly. "But a man with a serious problem might. Oh, Hillary, let's not talk about that until we've got more facts. If there was something wrong in Albert's life, it'll turn up soon enough. And that's probably where we'll find the motive for his murder."

"But what if the motive was burned up in the files at the winery?" She hadn't even thought about the fire until now, but it made perfect sense in this new context. "We may have already lost our chance to uncover the motive."

"That the fire was deliberate would make sense, wouldn't it?" Jeff admitted. "They'd burn all the files rather than steal the one they were worried about so that we wouldn't be able to figure out what's missing. But that would mean that the motive is business-related, wouldn't it?"

"I'd think so," Hillary said. The mystery that confronted them began to take hold of her imagination, pushing sorrow off to a safe distance, at least for the time being. "We'll have to go through the books with a fine-tooth comb. Maybe something will show up."

"Good idea. And I'll check with the police and see if they have anything new to add. We won't have the medical examiner's report for a couple days, but I don't think it will tell us anything that the police investigation didn't. I should get back to town, anyway. Are you going to be all right?"

"I'm fine," she said. "I'll need my car, though, won't I?" He'd taken her home in his from the police station the night before. She remembered that now.

"I'll bring it out," Jeff said, standing. "You take it easy. I had Emily bring some provisions on her way to the winery this morning. You've got eggs, milk and a loaf of bread to tide you over until you can shop for yourself. I think there was some sandwich meat, as well."

"Thank you."

"Nothing to it. Are you sure you're all right?" The concern in his eyes shone with a determined fire as he looked at her. She looked strangely fragile seated at the large maple table. Jeff wasn't accustomed to thinking of her as being so vulnerable. "I won't be gone long."

"I'm fine. You've got work to do. I may walk over to the winery and look through the books. In fact, I'll walk over to the winery in a bit and have Emily take me into town to get my car."

"It's no bother to bring it out."

"Don't bother. I want to go to town, anyway."

"All right," he agreed. "But don't push yourself too hard today. Emotional stress is sometimes more dangerous than physical trauma."

"Don't act like an old mother hen, Jeff." Hillary managed a smile as she stood to guide him to the door. She had the feeling that he would stay all day if she showed the least sign of wanting him to. But, at the moment, all she wanted was to be alone. "I'm tired right now. I think I'll eat something and then lie down. Maybe I'll wait awhile before I go."

"Good. I'll see you later."

It wasn't until after Jeff had driven away that Hillary allowed her anguished tears to flow freely. Albert's seemingly arbitrary death was so senseless that she couldn't react in any other way. Jeff was right, there was nothing that she could have done to stop it. She couldn't have done anything and could do nothing now. Nothing. It was hopeless.

Hopeless.

What had the man—was it really Jeff—said in her dream? Love was hopeless? Senseless.

The dream that brought her here and the dream she'd had this morning were both as senseless as Albert's death. Unconscious dread had transformed to images—that's all the dreams were. But why dream such things? And why dream a warning when it can't do any good?

If the past two days could turn out to be only an elaborate nightmare, she'd be the happiest woman alive. But that hope was probably the most senseless dream she'd had yet. And Hillary was a practical woman who knew that while tears provided a much-needed emotional release they didn't solve anything. The only way to find the truth about Albert's death was to pull herself together and look for it. With that in mind, she washed her face resolutely, changed into a blouse and comfortable knee-length skirt, and began to make a light meal from the groceries Jeff had had Emily bring to her. She would work through her sorrow somehow, and then she'd be ready to do something to straighten things out.

Emily had brought a package of sliced ham and a head of lettuce as well as the milk and eggs, so Hillary made a sandwich. She took her sandwich and a bottle of mineral water to the dining room. Just as she stepped through the door, she stopped.

What was that? A sound? Footsteps.

"Jeff? Is that you?"

Hillary put the food down on the dining room table carefully and approached the living room door nervously. What if someone was out there? No, she was only hearing things, wasn't she? She hadn't heard the door open, had she? There couldn't be anyone there. But she definitely heard another footstep on the hardwood living room floor.

"Who's there?" She stepped through the doorway and looked around the room. Nobody.

Then she saw him. In the far corner, obscured by the shadows imposed on the room by the drawn blinds, a man in a dark coat stood watching her. Her breath froze in her throat. She stared at him, fear and anger clenching her stomach.

"What do you want?" Hillary broke her frozen stance with the words. She stepped into the room, ready to grab the poker from the fireplace to defend herself. "Get out!" she shouted, only thinking then that the man who killed Albert might be after her. Coming into this room could have been the most foolish thing she'd ever done in her life!

He didn't answer but stepped out of the shadow and stopped, arms outstretched. Now she could see him more clearly, and the sight alarmed her more than the initial surprise had. He was the man from her dream! He wore a dark coat and a black hat. A bolo tie hung against his white shirt. He was definitely the same man she'd dreamed of. And he did look vaguely like Jeff! But who was he?

"Get out!" Forgetting any thought of self-defense, she slipped carefully to her left, toward the door to the solarium. She had to get away from this man! "Just leave me alone!" Her voice quavered with icy fear, her muscles protesting her efforts to move slowly toward safety.

The man walked quickly now, moving to cut off her retreat. His expression was twisted by some inner anguish, his hands out and reaching for her. He seemed to be in such pain that she almost stopped, in sympathy for his obvious sorrow. But she kept moving.

"No," she said. "Get out! I'll call the cops. Get out of my house!" She was almost to the door, almost free... he would be slowed by the couch. If she could just get her legs to run, she'd be safe. But icy tendrils of fear were reaching down from the back of her neck as though to freeze her movements. If she didn't run now, she felt she never would.

With a savage cry, Hillary threw herself at the door. The man seemed to fly at her. He crossed the room faster than humanly possible and grasped her shoulder with a cool hand just as she threw the door open and tumbled through. Falling onto the flagstones, in the glare of sunlight that filled the solarium, she rolled to stare back at her pursuer.

He stepped through the door. But when the sunlight struck him, he dissolved. A rush of cool air flowed over her and was gone.

Hillary's breath caught in her throat. That couldn't have happened! Couldn't have. Yesterday she'd imagined a voice, and now she was imagining intruders. She knew she'd rather be hallucinating than to have what she'd just seen be true. When she finally did draw a breath, it was with a ragged gasp of fear and astonishment. She laid flat on the sun-heated floor and closed her eyes, vowing not to open them until she'd thought of some rational reason for what she'd just seen.

There was no rational reason except that she was insane. Either that, or she'd just seen a ghost. That thought left her shivering in the warm sunlight of the solarium—shivering with icy fear.

Chapter Three

Hillary's first impulse was to leap to her feet and call Jeff to tell him what had just happened. But she remained frozen, incredulously immobile, trying to slow her breath down so that she could think. What if it wasn't just a "vision"? What if it was something more than that? Was he waiting for her to come back inside?

She had no experience to tell her what to do next. Nothing she knew of could have prepared her for something this bizarre, so she sat very still and peered into the dim living room. There was no harm in waiting. Jeff had only just left, so he wasn't in his office to receive her call, anyway.

After a moment that seemed to last hours, Hillary forced herself to relax. Whatever the thing was, paranormal spirit or hallucination, it had disappeared as soon as it hit the sunlight flooding the solarium, so she was obviously quite safe here. As for the inside of the house? Well, it was her house and she'd have to go in sooner or later.

Hillary stood and smoothed her hair, a look of determination growing on her regally expressive face. *It may have been the shock. You're imagining things because of the stress you're going through right now.*

That was it. She hadn't seen anything. It just wasn't possible. In her current state of mind, it was understandable that she would take the image of disorder from her dream and impose it on her waking world.

It made sense, of course, but it was still hard to step over the threshold and into the house proper. Once inside, she wasted no time in opening the drapes to let in a flood of sunlight. It bathed the room in safe yellow light.

Now, what should her next move be? Obviously, the most important thing to do would be to check the winery records for any discrepancies. But first she'd need a shower and a change of clothing to get her started on the right foot.

Running the water in her spacious shower, Hillary slipped under the fine spray and let the warmth soak through her. Relaxing beneath the massaging flow of water, Hillary was finally able to begin sorting through last night's events. The image of Albert sitting on the couch in his office was only a dim memory to her, but then she hadn't been in the room long before Jeff guided her out in his sheltering arms. The majority of her time at Albert's home had been spent either in the kitchen talking to a young officer or sitting alone feeling utterly helpless. It had been Jeff who stayed with the policemen when they examined the crime scene, and Jeff who knew the details. For Hillary, the evening was a moment of horror followed by a seemingly endless and mind-numbing contemplation of that horror.

She only vaguely remembered Jeff taking her home later, but she didn't remember arriving here. Though she might have done quite well without Jeff, she was extremely glad that he'd been there for her. It was during the bad times that a person needed friends like Jeff Simpson.

He hadn't wanted to tell her what the police had said about Albert, today. She could tell that he'd wanted to shelter her. His concern for her was sweetly reassuring, and it was a constant in her life.

Hillary left the warm shower reluctantly and wrapped one of her oversize bath towels around her lithe body. She used another towel to rub her hair with life-affirming vigor. Now she felt human again. And, after quickly blowing her hair dry and clothing herself in a trim denim skirt and simple white blouse, she felt ready to face the world again.

When she crossed the living room this time, she felt no lingering trepidation. It was just her mind playing tricks on her after her shock. Time and concentration on the task at hand would take care of that.

"HILLARY, YOU POOR DEAR, sit down! My God, girl, you should be home, not coming in here today of all days!" Emily Pragger greeted Hillary with an effusive rush of words and then grasped her in a consoling hug. The two stepped into the winery office. Emily, a large woman in her late fifties with kind blue eyes and a constant smile, looked worn out herself, but she seemed to mask her feelings in deference to Hillary's pain. "You don't have to be here, you know," she continued. "Anything that needs doing can wait a day or two."

"I know," Hillary admitted when the older woman broke their embrace. "But I couldn't sit at home. It's all such a shock."

"I know. Jeff called me first thing this morning so I wouldn't hear it from someone on the street. I still don't believe it. Albert never offended anyone that I know of. Not to that extreme, at least."

"I don't understand it, either."

They were still standing near the door. Emily grasped Hillary's shoulders and regarded her with motherly concern.

"I guess that's why I'm here now," Hillary said. "It's better that I find something to do. I can't just sit around wondering what happened. Maybe I could clean out those burned files."

"I took care of that already," Emily said. "I guess I needed something extra to occupy myself with this morning, too."

"Then I guess you know why I'm here."

"Yes, yes. Well, come on in and get some coffee." She led the way to the coffeemaker on an oak mission table beside the window overlooking the vineyards. "You do still drink coffee, don't you? I think we've got some mineral water, if you don't."

"Coffee would be great," she said, even though she usually drank decaf. Looking around the bright office now, Hillary could hardly believe that there had been a fire there the night before. Other than the blackened wall behind the file cabinets, everything else seemed to be in order.

"Here you go, dear. You still take it black, don't you?"

"Yes, I do." Hillary accepted the cup and followed Emily to her desk and sat across from her. "I thought we weren't supposed to run the power until everything was checked."

"It's all taken care of, dear." Emily nodded over her cup, her lively eyes dancing over Hillary's face in appraisal. "I had Dale Hanken, our insurance man, come out here bright and early. And the electrician came right on his heels. That fire didn't stop us any."

"What did the electrician have to say about the wiring? Is it okay?" Hillary's coffee was hot and strong, a well-remembered taste she'd nearly forgotten after years of drinking decaf.

"One hundred percent. He figures it was only a bad receptacle, though it was hard to tell from what was left of it."

"Did he think the computer caused it to get hot? The machine was running."

"Running? What do you mean?" Emily cocked her head at Hillary, a quizzical look in her eye.

"It was still switched on when I was here," Hillary said. "I assumed that it had either made the plug heat, or that one of those old survey maps had fallen behind the cabinets, across the blades of the plug."

"The computer wasn't on when I left yesterday, dear," Emily said, concern tightening her brows. "I'm as certain as I can be about that."

"The switch was on when I checked last night. It didn't have any power but it was on."

"In twenty-five years, I've never left anything running that shouldn't be when I've gone home for the night," Emily said defensively. "I don't see why I would have last night."

"Maybe someone else used it later. Was Albert in?"

"I don't know, though he might have been," the other woman admitted. "He wasn't in at all during the day yesterday."

"Where was he?"

"I don't know," Emily said. "He left at noon the day before and didn't come in yesterday."

"You said on the phone that he'd been out of the office more often than before. You meant like yesterday?" Hillary didn't feel like questioning Albert's working habits at the moment, but that might be exactly the information that was needed to find his killer.

"Yes. Lord knows he didn't have to account to me for his time, but I would have appreciated some word about where he could be reached. On the other hand, the business isn't so large that it can't run itself for the most part. He had every right to do as he pleased."

"Certainly," Hillary agreed.

"What's the point in owning the business if you're going to let yourself be chained to it?" Emily spoke sadly, thinking, perhaps, of happier days and wondering what course life would follow after this dramatic breaking point. "Anyway, what does it matter now where he was?"

"I don't know. But Albert's behavior was never so erratic in the past, so I've been thinking that his absences may be related to his death."

"In what way?"

"I don't know that, either." Hillary shrugged, sipping her coffee. "How long had he been keeping this loose work schedule?"

"Oh, six months, maybe. No more than that."

"Was he nervous at all?"

"No more than usual," Emily said. "You know Albert. He was very particular about things."

"Yes, he was. Which makes his recent behavior all the less understandable. Where did he go in San Francisco?"

"I don't know."

It was clear from the expression of regret on Emily's face that he hadn't confided in her and that lack of confidence had hurt her. She'd been working for the winery in one capacity or another for over twenty-five years, and she'd earned that much.

"I sure wish I knew something that would help," she said now. "But I just don't."

"SO TRAGIC," PROCLAIMED Franz Hunt, their winemaker, as he greeted Hillary with a warm embrace. "Just when young Albert was beginning to relax a bit and enjoy life, he was cut down. Tragic. And you, Hillary—to come back to this must be horrible."

"Yes," she said, returning the older man's sad smile, "I didn't even have a chance to see him. I didn't know where he was."

"Yes, well, as I said, Albert was apparently determined to be less of the workaholic these past few months," Franz said, leading her past three large stainless steel wine vats and into his small office. "He was often away from the vineyards."

"Do you know where he went, Franz?" Hillary accepted a seat in a chair near the stacked reports that were used to track the condition of the grapes. "Do you know what he did?"

"Why do you ask such things? He's dead, Hillary. It makes no difference now." Franz shook his head, his craggy face long with remorse.

"But it may, Franz." Hillary spoke with an urgent tone that enlivened her voice, hoping that this man might know what Emily hadn't. "He isn't just dead. He was murdered. And his routine during the past couple months might give us some clue about who did it."

"It's best to leave that to the police," Franz advised.

"No!" Hillary said vehemently. "I can't sit and wait for someone else to investigate. I'll go crazy if I do that."

"But, Hillary, what can you do? You are not a law officer. You cannot arrest anyone."

"No, but I can at least try to figure this thing out."

"I don't know if I can be of much help, but I can certainly try if you are so set on this."

"I am. Do you know where he went?"

"Not precisely." Franz sat on the edge of the worn old desk that dominated his cluttered office, his lips pursed in thought. "I do know he went to San Francisco many times. He always seemed to be in such a terrible hurry, as if he were dissatisfied with something but didn't know what to do about it."

"Dissatisfied?"

"Yes. Or nervous, perhaps."

"Wasn't he happy?"

"I think he was, Hillary. He laughed quite a lot, at any rate."

"Laughed? Out loud?" That wasn't like Albert. Not that he was unusually dour, but he wasn't the type to laugh aloud at many things. Not easily, anyway.

"Oh, yes," Franz confirmed. "But then there were times when he became quite snappish. That is why I feel he was dissatisfied."

"I see. And this was in the last few months?"

"Yes, I would say so."

"And he began paying less attention to business at about the same time?"

"Yes, but I wouldn't judge him harshly on that matter. This is a small winery. Our business is all a matter of long-standing form. Until we begin the harvest, there is little for a manager to do.''

"I wasn't judging him, Franz. I'd told him he should take things easier, myself."

"So you see, he finally took your advice."

"Maybe. But it still seems wrong, somehow." Hillary couldn't think of anything else to ask on the matter. If Albert had found a diversion in San Francisco, she'd probably never be able to find out what it was. "He was snappish sometimes?"

"Yes. Perhaps he was preoccupied."

"It wasn't like him to act that way."

"There is no way to know what is in a man's mind."

"No, I guess not."

"It may have been that he was unlucky at cards on those occasions," Franz suggested.

"What, in the poker game?" Albert had played poker with several local men every Friday night for years, but they'd always been penny-ante games. He wasn't a good player, but then he wasn't the kind to take a loss to heart, either.

"I think perhaps they upped the stakes lately. Or maybe there was another game going."

"I'll check with Jeff," Hillary said. "But I can't see their little game being the cause of any problems."

"As I say, I don't know for sure. But it is a possibility."

"I certainly doubt a poker game led to his death."

"Of course not," Franz said, shock registering in his voice. "One does not kill someone over a few dollars lost among friends."

"I know. I'm afraid that if there is a connection to his death, it will be in San Francisco."

"Yes, and we don't know where he went except to the city."

"Maybe we could find out, though. His credit-card receipts should tell us something."

"Yes, if his trips were company business," Franz said. "He wouldn't have used them for personal reasons."

"I'd forgotten," Hillary said, disheartened. Albert was a stickler for accountability. And, for personal use, he favored cash. "Of course, he wasn't a fool. So he wouldn't have taken large amounts of cash with him. His checkbook may be what I want."

"It may be. Still, I don't think you should investigate. You are only torturing yourself, my dear."

"No, it would be torture to do nothing, Franz. I've never been good at waiting."

SHE WAS BEAUTIFUL!

He was watching her as she walked from the winery to the office, marveling at the shapely curve of leg showing beneath her short skirt. She walked with such authority, such obvious command, that he was mesmerized by her mere movement across the short expanse of yard between the buildings. He found her so beautiful!

Albert's death was unavoidable, of course, though it troubled him that she didn't understand the complete facts of that matter. He surely couldn't have kept Albert from dying. Only Albert could have done that, and Albert himself hadn't known enough to try. What troubled him now was not Albert's death but the pain she felt over it. She shouldn't have to suffer such sadness, but he didn't know how to console her. His attempt to approach her openly had been a disaster. All he could do now was watch and wait.

Only after she had entered the office did he dare cross the parking lot to the building. As important as it was that she not see him, it was equally important that he keep her in sight. He wasn't about to lose her again.

HILLARY STOPPED INSIDE the door, turned swiftly and threw it open again.

Nothing. She could have sworn there had been movement outside, but no one was there now. There was no place to hide in the parking lot or in the grass bordering it, either.

Obviously, she'd been mistaken. Still, even as she walked along the hall to Emily's office, she couldn't shake the feeling that she was being watched. It wasn't until she was in the office with the other woman that she felt secure again.

"You look pale, dear." Emily half rose behind her desk, concern stamped on her face. "Did something happen?"

"No, I—oh, nothing." Hillary smiled. It was just her foolish nerves, after all. "Did Albert still keep his old check registers here at the office?"

"Checks? I think so. Why?" Emily sat again.

"I was thinking they might give us a clue about where he went in San Francisco. Where did he keep them?"

"Why, in the—" Emily stopped abruptly, her gaze moving from Hillary to the fire-damaged file cabinets. "In the files."

"The files? Oh, that can't be coincidental, Emily. The fire was just too convenient to be a coincidence."

Hillary wondered what else among the supposedly harmless paperwork had been important enough to destroy. Had his killer obliterated evidence with the fire? And, if so, could she still find a way to get him?

One thing was certain, she'd have to move quickly if she was going to succeed.

SHE'D ALMOST SEEN HIM! He hadn't thought it was possible, but she must have seen something. She'd surprised him by throwing the door open and peering out with such fear in her eyes. He hadn't meant to scare her. Not her, not for any reason. Fortunately, she'd returned to her task inside apparently satisfied that she was alone.

Standing as she had, shaded by the building from the sun's direct rays, she'd looked just as he remembered her. Her eyes were the most splendid shade of green he'd ever seen, her lips full yet strong. She was a woman of character, strength and intelligence. Dear God, he had to have her back.

This time, no one would stop him from joining her. This time, there was no way they could.

Chapter Four

"Did you and Albert still play poker every Friday night?"

Hillary pulled a chair up beside Jeff. She'd found him at the keyboard of one of the video terminals at the newspaper. He'd been so absorbed in his work that he hadn't noticed her approaching and he jumped visibly when she placed her hand on his shoulder. Then he looked up, smiling brightly.

"Poker?" he said now. "Not regularly. Albert and I were the only bachelors left in the group, and the guys usually had better things to do on Friday night than play cards."

"Those wedding bells are breaking up that old gang of yours, huh?" she teased with a gentle smile.

"If I was married I sure wouldn't waste every Friday playing cards, either," he said. "It was mostly just a way to kill an empty evening, anyway. None of us were really any good at the game."

"Are there any other poker games going on in town?"

"I'd imagine that lots of people play cards every now and again." Jeff tilted his head slightly, appraising her in the same careful manner he always had when wondering what she was up to. Growing up with Hillary had given him a deep appreciation for her ability to surprise him. "Why are you so interested in poker?"

"I don't know if I actually am," she admitted. She'd come to town feeling rushed and agitated, but as usual Jeff's presence had a calming effect on her. Being with Jeff always made Hillary feel as though she could afford to take a deep breath and relax. And now that she had, she realized that she was running off in all directions at once. "It's just that—well, Albert was killed for some reason. I know that poker is a long shot, but it's still a possibility."

"Our little game?" Jeff was incredulous.

"No," Hillary said quickly. "But Franz suggested that Albert might have played in another game as well. He might have fallen in with a more intense group of card players."

"Not in St. Helena," Jeff said. "The town isn't large enough that a regular game would be going on without my hearing about it. Besides, I'm sure that Albert would have mentioned it."

"I thought as much. It was a slim hope, anyway."

"Really, Hillary, it would seem to be very slim. Albert never won at cards, not when I played with him. Face it, nobody would kill the loser."

"No, they wouldn't." Hillary sat quietly for a moment and considered her remaining avenues of exploration.

"So, what are you thinking of now, Hill?" Jeff broke in on her thoughts. Her hand rested on her crossed legs and he reached to pat it gently.

"San Francisco," she said. "Albert was making a lot of trips to San Francisco in the last few months. I'm wondering what he was doing there."

"That could be tough to find out," Jeff said. "Do you have any credit card slips or bills to go by? Returned checks?"

"I don't know. He kept his check registers at work. I'm afraid they burned in the fire. I'm on my way to his house to see if I can find his checkbook now. He might have some credit card bills there."

"There you go, then," Jeff said hopefully. "You can't spend much time in the big city without spending money. There's got to be some record of it."

"Yes, but Albert generally restricted his cards to business expenses, and those trips don't appear to have been business. But then I don't suppose I'll know until I go and look."

"I'd volunteer to come help you, but I'm in a bit of a bind," Jeff said, his brows knit in a pensive frown. "After all, this is a news story, and I can't just go off the record with everything."

"I know, Jeff, and I appreciate all that you've done so far." Hillary grasped his arm, giving it an appreciative squeeze. "I wouldn't want you to compromise your position on my account. And I imagine you've already put yourself behind on your own work."

"No, the only benefit of being the editor is that I can send other people out to do the stories."

"Then you aren't covering the murder yourself?"

"No, I've put Gil Dickinson on it. Murder is more his line than mine, anyway."

"He'll write a good piece, I'm sure," Hillary said, though she'd have preferred for Jeff to have written it himself. It was always best to keep tragedy in the family.

"Is there anything else I can help you with?"

"No, not right now." Hillary stood. "I'm going to see if I can get into Albert's house. There may be something there that the police missed."

"Just try to remember that the police are doing their best, Hill," Jeff cautioned her. "You don't win any friends butting heads with Chief McDonald."

"I'm not looking to win friends," Hillary stated seriously. "I want to find out why my cousin was killed and who did it."

"Which is what the cops want as well. Just don't try to take over their investigation."

"Jeff, I—"

"Hey, Hillary, don't start playing innocent with me." Jeff laughed. "You're a go-getter, Hillary, but that attitude will look like meddling to the police."

"I know. And I won't step on any toes, I assure you. Do you know if the house is sealed off?"

"Yes, it is." Jeff stood, walking her to the door. "But I'm sure that isn't meant to keep you out. They'll want you to go through everything as soon as possible, anyway, I'd imagine."

"I'll stop by the police station first, then." Pausing at the door, she grasped her friend's arm softly and smiled. "I want to thank you again for staying with me last night. I couldn't have stood waking alone."

"Forget about it, Hill." Jeff's hand rose automatically. He stroked two fingers down her cheek and smiled wistfully. "Your car is in the lot. Keys over the sun visor. You take care of yourself, okay?"

"Right. I'll call you later."

Jeff watched her walk away from the newspaper, his smile frozen on his lean face. She was an impressive woman in every respect, and at this moment the feelings he held for her welled up within him. It was harder than ever to maintain his composure in her presence, especially now when he wanted to do nothing but console her in her grief.

The thought of her having to deal with this unexpected loss alone gave him a cold pain in the pit of his stomach. The death of her father had been tough on her, but there had been time to prepare for that. This, however, was something straight out of left field and it had hit her like a bomb. He could never have left her alone in that condition. Never.

Of course, she wasn't the kind of woman who needed help facing adversity. Strong and independent, Hillary attacked life with both fists and was always up to any challenge. He was sure that she was up to this challenge, too. He wondered if he would hold up this well under similar circumstances.

Closing the door, Jeff returned to his terminal pondering the vagaries of life. Death came more quickly than most people thought—as quickly as going to sleep really—and that thought caused him to shiver even in the summer heat. Mortality was too close in normal times, but to have someone actively dealing out death was something he didn't care to contemplate. Not when it might be Hillary who came under the killer's sights next.

He keyed-off the piece he'd been writing. His mind wasn't on his work any longer, and because his was a weekly paper, he had plenty of time before his deadline. He went into his office and closed the door. Sitting at his desk, he stared absently at the old photograph on the wall across from him.

"Well, Victor," he said to the man in the photograph. "Your newspaper is doing most of its printing in red ink these days, and all the editor can think of is a woman. A most wonderful woman, to be sure, but I should be giving more attention to keeping the rag on the stands. Or should I?''

He smiled, shaking his head. Somehow, the more the financial condition of the paper worsened, the more the man in the photograph seemed to sympathize with his plight. The man's severe expression seemed to soften slightly, though Jeff knew it was only a trick of light. Victor Simpson had founded the paper over a hundred years ago, and Jeffery Simpson was going to lose it now if he couldn't come up with the money for a new press. Victor would surely not be sympathetic if he were alive to say his piece.

The newspaper had come to Jeff's great-grandfather after Victor's premature death in a riding accident, and it had done well over time. Until now, that is. Newspapers were no longer a steady business, especially not small weeklies. If he could afford a new color press, he could put them in the black with outside printing orders. But he couldn't do that without an extension on his credit, something the bank was in no position to offer at the moment. Times were tough all over.

But Jeff hadn't come into his office to fret over that just now. He had another mission in mind, and so he removed a copy of the San Francisco yellow pages from the shelf and paged through it quickly.

"You in, Jeff?" Gil Dickinson knocked on the door. He opened it and entered without waiting for Jeff's reply.

"Yeah, I'm in, Gil." Jeff grinned without looking up, holding his finger beneath a phone number as he copied it down on a notepad. Then he closed the phone book and pushed it aside. "What did you get?"

"A headache, mostly." Gil sat across the desk and pulled his notebook from the inner pocket of his sport coat. "But I do have the beginning of a story. Now, if you ran a daily, we might have a fine little running story to help pull this rag out of the red."

"Right, Gil." Jeff laughed. "Of course, I could cut your salary to improve our balance sheet as well."

"A cut in my salary would involve me paying you, I think." Gil ran his hand through his steel-gray hair and laughed. He'd started at *The Napa Press* forty years earlier before becoming a *New York Times* police reporter. When he'd retired from the *Times* at sixty-two, he'd returned to St. Helena and to the *Press*.

"It was a single shot," Gil said, turning his attention to his pad. "They're guessing that it was a .38 caliber, but we won't know until after the autopsy."

"When will that be?"

"They should be nearly finished by now," he said, checking his watch. "It'll be a couple days before the complete results are in."

"Did you get something else?"

"Nothing definite." Gil paused, scratching at his jaw with the knuckles of his right hand. "I tell you, though, it looks screwy."

"How so?"

"Hell, I saw the pictures. I saw the office. I don't have to be a cop to draw my own conclusions." Then he stopped again, regarding Jeff with calm consideration.

"And they are?"

"Well my conclusions are screwy, too, I'm afraid." Gil frowned. "But everything looks like suicide, Jeffery. Everything."

"Except that there was no weapon."

"Yes, that does damage the theory a bit, I'll admit. But I can't for the life of me see how everything could look like it does and still be murder."

"Come on, Gil, being shot in the mouth doesn't naturally mean suicide."

"I know, but there are many small things." Gil opened his notebook again and flipped a couple pages back. "One telling thing is the pattern of blood spattered on his hand."

"He was trying to get the gun away from his killer," Jeff countered, desperate to discount the other man's theory, for Hillary's sake.

"But only one hand was bloody. And the middle of his right index finger is bloodless, even though the rest of his hand was well covered. It would seem to have been protected by the trigger guard at the time of the shot."

"But not necessarily."

"Hell, Jeff, nothing is certain. But there was no evident struggle."

"And no evident weapon."

"Right, but the police are looking for a blue steel Smith & Wesson .38."

"Why?"

"Albert had the revolver registered in his name, but it's missing. The gun case is empty."

"Do they have any ideas about how the gun came to be missing?"

"They figure that the murderer took it with him." Gil slowly smiled.

"The murderer took it?" Jeff smiled, too. "So, your suicide theory isn't held universally."

"No, but we've got a week of developments yet before we hit the stands, junior, so nothing is settled yet."

Gil stood, still smiling. "Of course, I won't complain if I'm wrong. Albert was a good guy. And he sure as hell had no reason to kill himself. Besides, murder sells more papers."

"Oh, that's hard, Gil." Jeff rocked back in his chair, the smile leaving his face. "But true enough. Go make up your piece and leave me alone."

"Right."

The older man left the office as quickly as he had entered, leaving Jeff alone. Suicide? He hadn't liked that thought when it first came up, and he liked it even less now that Gil shared it. As careful with conversation as he was with his writing, Gil Dickinson wasn't the type to announce his theories if he didn't feel pretty sure of them.

Still, Albert hadn't removed the gun from the room. But who did?

HILLARY WAITED VERY impatiently in Chief Mc-Donald's outer office. His secretary had left after telling Hillary that the chief was on the phone and would be with her in a moment.

The room was small and plain, with a short couch and a secretary's desk. It wasn't a pleasant place to wait. Its stark walls were punctuated only by police citations, and Hillary was tempted just to go out to Albert's house without talking to the chief first. But she knew better than to ruffle official feathers. No, she'd talk to the chief and follow all the protocol, but she didn't have to like it.

Hillary closed her eyes. She felt tired, drained by the effort it took to continue walking around with the burden of her grief on her shoulders. Thoughts of the many times she'd laughed with Albert as well as the many times he'd annoyed her kept slipping into her mind.

They had been close, yet distant, two very different personalities that complemented each other in the family business. Hillary's outgoing, hard-driven nature was destined to take her away in search of greater challenges, while Albert's studied, calm attitude predisposed him to remain in the valley. That calm had often seemed like inertia to Hillary, and she had chided Albert on occasion. He would only smile, secure with his choices and content with his place in the world.

Perhaps it was his unsettled youth that gave him his appreciation of a calm, well-ordered life. His parents, Hillary's Uncle Phillip and his wife, Marjorie, had traveled extensively on winery business, moving Albert from school to school. He'd never had a real home until he'd come to live with Hillary and her father during his senior year of high school. Then a plane crash had taken his parents' lives. After that, Albert had stayed at the family base in the Napa Valley. He'd left only long enough to study enology and business at UCLA.

It was Hillary who'd left to take over the role of family financial manager that Phillip de Gaetano had filled. In all fairness to her jet-setting uncle, the family had set up their business in the financial markets mostly as a fallback to help the wine business through market slumps. As such, it hadn't required very much attention from Phillip.

Hillary, on the other hand, was a determined hands-on manager, and she had steered them into a steady profit position. Just as Albert had been the cornerstone of their efforts to expand their winemaking, Hillary had been the driving force behind their success on the East Coast. Together, each in their own way, Albert and Hillary had brought de Gaetano Enterprises into the nineties.

Yes, they'd been a good team. But that was all over now, and Hillary couldn't help but feel pessimistic about the future. Through some twist of fate, the de Gaetano family now had only one lone survivor. Hillary had become accustomed to managing, but that had been in partnership with Albert. Now she not only had to manage the whole operation herself, but she had to face the fact that, after her, the de Gaetano family name would be gone. She was the end of the line.

The end of the line.

All gone now.

She could hear the voice from her dream as clearly as though the man was speaking into her ear in an ominous whisper.

It's all gone. Don't fret, darling. Nothing lasts forever, and you'll see that things will work out for the best.

The voice was clear and close and speaking words that didn't come from her dream. The mind, Hillary thought, is a very strange place.

Come to me, darling. Come and rest. We'll decipher it all tomorrow. Come to me, love, and I'll help you.

That wasn't right. She hadn't dreamed anything like that. Hillary opened her eyes, confusion creasing her forehead. Then she sat up with a sharp intake of breath and stared ahead in mute shock.

The man was standing in front of her, leaning slightly toward her and smiling. His dark coat was dusty and the hat he held in his hands was spotted by rain. For a moment, he was crystal clear, his brown hair creased by his hat, his gray eyes looking at her hopefully. Then he faded just as he had in her home, evaporating until she found herself staring at the beige wall. Fear crept up her spine. She was still staring, barely breathing, when Chief McDonald opened his door.

"Miss de Gaetano?"

"What?" She jumped. Then, realizing how that must have looked to him, she forced a smile to her lips and took a deep breath. Her legs were shaking slightly as she stood, but they supported her well enough. "Hello, Chief," she said, her voice quavering slightly.

"Come in," the police officer said. "I'm sorry to have kept you waiting, but I'm afraid everything is off schedule around here. Come on in and sit down."

She followed him into his office, pausing at the door to look back at the couch she'd occupied a moment before. There was nothing there and, most likely, there never had been anything. Her visitor was an illusion, the trick of a shocked mind. Jeff was right; her grief was more deeply felt than any physical pain she could imagine.

"We checked out your fire," he said. "Looks like possible arson. We can't really be certain since we don't know if the computer was plugged in all the way. If it wasn't, we don't know what might have been lying across the prongs of the plug. The electrician tells us that the computer wasn't damaged, so it wasn't an overload in the machine. But there was no evidence of gasoline or any other accelerant for the flames. Might just be a fluke. We'll do everything we can."

"I'm sure you will, Chief," she said, surprised at how calm she sounded. "I came over to offer my help."

"We could use a bit, that's certain. You would know more than I about Albert's personal affairs, after all.

We need someone to look through his effects and see if there is anything there to help us.''

"That's what I was planning to do." Hillary crossed her legs and folded her hands on top of her knee, regarding the man in a studious manner that had carried her through many tense business meetings. Knowing that she looked externally calm helped to calm her internally, and though she might be allowed a bit of emotion just now, she wanted to maintain as much control as possible. "Obviously, Albert's death didn't occur without cause, and I'd like to find out why he was killed.''

"Of course.''

"Is the house open now?'' she asked. "I'd like to look at his things as soon as possible.''

"Not just yet, Miss de Gaetano." McDonald frowned, tapping his desktop with one nervous finger. "I've called for a forensic expert from the state police, and we'd like to give him a chance at the scene of the crime before we do any more there.''

"But I needn't disturb the office,'' she said.

"Yes, but we'd like to keep the entire house sealed for the time being. You can't be sure where the clues are.''

"Goodness, Chief, your men were all over the place last night,'' she protested, incredulous that he would sanction any delay in the investigation. "Officers, ambulance attendants, myself, Jeff—we were all there, ruining the scene of the crime. I don't see the point—''

"Just the same, we'll leave it be until the state boys are done. Really, Miss de Gaetano, you can have free reign of the place by tomorrow afternoon.''

"That long!" Hillary gripped the arms of her chair in an effort to stifle her sudden anger. "His killer could be miles away by then. We might never—"

"No, his killer must be here in town. Albert never traveled any farther than San Francisco, and any business he conducted took place right here. You don't have to worry about the killer getting away."

"You can't be sure the murderer isn't from San Francisco!"

"No, but if he is then he probably feels quite safe staying put right there. And if he's local, he doesn't dare leave for fear that he'll draw attention to himself."

"Come now, we can certainly cover more than one thing at a time," Hillary managed.

"After the forensic people are finished," he said, his voice tightening around his resolve. "Then we'll go full bore, but I can't risk contaminating the scene any more than we already have. Besides, you've got the office records to look through. That's every bit as important as his home records."

"Sure, except that our little fire destroyed a good portion of those records, not to mention many of Albert's personal records."

"Which should tell you how important it is to look there first," McDonald said. "Believe me, I want you to be in on this investigation right along with us. And you can help us most by checking things at the winery. The killer couldn't have removed all the clues, and we'll find them wherever they are."

It was obvious that she was not going to get into the house today, so Hillary forced herself to relax a bit and accept that fact. Sealing the entire house now was like locking the barn door after the horse had been stolen, but if that was how they were going to play it, it was beyond her capability to change their plans. The most important rule of business was to know when to wait, and this was the time.

"All right," she said, standing. "I'll see if there's anything else I can do at the winery. You will call me as soon as I can enter the house, won't you?"

"Definitely." He stood. "We want your help on this. It's best that we investigate together. From what I hear, we probably couldn't have kept you out of Albert's place, anyway."

"What do you mean?"

"Oh, I spoke to Jeff Simpson, and he mentioned your intention to conduct your own inquiry. I don't blame you one bit." He shrugged good-naturedly as he walked around to open the door for her. "Please take some time to think of anything Albert may have said that might have bearing on the case. Anything at all, mind you, no matter how small it may seem. You do that and look through your winery records, and I'll call as soon as you can get into the house. Okay?"

"Okay," she said. "I'll be waiting."

"Goodbye."

She turned away, her calm dribbling away with each step as she considered his obvious maneuver to placate her with the task of checking the winery records. He didn't want her to be part of anything. He just wanted her out of the way. And worst of all, he all but told her that Jeff had called to warn him of her intentions. Her friend Jeffery had apparently decided that the best way to help her was to insulate her from the whole mess. That kind of help wasn't what she wanted from a friend. Hillary hadn't gotten this far in the world by being insulated, and she wasn't about to start letting people shelter her now.

THE HOUSE HAD STOOD on the slope of the valley for over a hundred years. Once a grand mansion at the center of a prosperous vineyard, the Foche house was a local landmark. It was still pointed out on the many tours of wine country that made their way over the valley's winding roads. But the grandeur the house had once held was gone now. Time and disuse had reduced it to nothing more than a curiosity. Not even the local high school students would go into it now; the dry rot had made its once-polished floors hazardous to anyone heavier than the mice that lived in its walls and the foxes that hunted the mice.

The Foche mansion only stood because Bernard Foche didn't want to spend the money it would cost to tear it down. Instead of removing the hazard, he had posted no-trespassing signs, nailed boards over the doors and lower windows and left it to rot in the shelter of its old oak trees. The place stood near his vines on the eastern slope of the valley. No one had been harmed there yet, and Bernard Foche was willing to gamble that there would be no injuries in the future. Besides, sooner or later, a lightning strike would reduce it to a flaming ruin, and the volunteer fire department would rush out to stand guard while nature did his demolition work for him.

Today, however, for the first time in a long time, the house had a visitor. The man walked quickly up from the vines and stood for a moment beneath the sprawling arms of an oak tree. The rotting wood of the porch windows could no longer hold nails, and the boards designed to keep people out had fallen to the ground, allowing free access.

The man used the front window to get in. He stepped carefully into the house and proceeded with equal care to the staircase and up to the second floor. The third step broke under his weight and the house's current occupants scurried beneath the steps.

Holding the remnant of the railing, the man continued up, testing each step as he went. Surprisingly, the rest of the steps were sound enough to hold him and the upper floor was in better condition than he'd expected it to be.

He hurried to what had been a large bedroom and went directly to an old trunk; it rested against one wall near a broken bed frame and rusted springs. He lifted the lid, the old leather straps doing very little to secure it to the trunk after so many seasons exposed to the elements. Holding the lid half open, he reached beneath his jacket, removed a blue steel revolver from the waistband of his slacks and dropped it into the trunk. Then he replaced the lid and retraced his steps. He was relieved to have gotten in and out without going through the floor.

He didn't look back as he returned to the rows of grapevines hanging heavy with fruit. The house didn't concern him now that his mission there was finished. It would keep his secret just as it kept its many other secrets, and its eventual decay would carry the weapon down to the ground, to be buried as part of the unknown history of the house in the vineyard.

Reaching a dirt road, the man got into his car and started the engine. Only then did he look back toward the house. For a moment, just the briefest sliver of time, he'd thought he could see a man in a black coat standing beneath the old oak trees. There was no one there, of course, but the image remained as he stepped on the gas and roared away.

For a moment, he could swear that he had heard the man laughing.

Chapter Five

Hillary drove onto the winery grounds in a better state of mind than that with which she'd left the police station. The drive along the road that slowly wound up from St. Helena and the valley floor to her own land had always served to relax her. The countryside was lush this time of year, and even during the long drought the valley was rich with ripe, full vines. She knew that the appearance was deceptive, of course, for the grapes weren't nearly as full as they would be in a good year.

On this visit to the winery office, Hillary wasn't distracted by grief or confusion. This time she had a purpose and a steady determination to check every possible place where Albert might have left a clue. There must be something to explain what was going on in his life over the past couple months. Because of the fire in the file cabinets, it was certain that there would be no obvious clues. It would only be by piecing together the many small clues that she would be able to solve the mystery.

The office of the de Gaetano winery was deceptively small for a company that distributed its product nationwide. But, though de Gaetano wines graced tables from California to Maine to Florida, the vineyard itself was still not much more than a large family farm, and the necessary bookkeeping had been handled easily by Albert, Emily and the assistant, June Dayton, who came three afternoons a week.

The entire business was operated from two offices attached to the front of a mission-style building that, in turn, housed the large vats where the grapes were put through their first fermentation. The main office was a twelve-by-fifteen-foot room containing Emily's and June's desks, as well as the files of sales and crop reports. Some of the papers dated back to the 1860s, when Alberto de Gaetano had brought his vines from Italy and started the vineyard. Fortunately, the historical papers were not kept with those containing current paperwork and so had not been damaged by the fire.

The job information concerning current employees had burned. The tax forms and payroll records had all been totally destroyed along with, unfortunately, some of Albert's personal accounting records.

Hillary was counting on finding duplicate records. Most of the files were also stored in the company's computer. She didn't expect to find personal records in the computer, but Albert had been a meticulous man and it was possible. That was Hillary's hope, anyway.

It was shortly after six o'clock when she unlocked the front door and entered the office. Franz had apparently gone home, as had the vineyard foreman. The absence of people brought back the foreboding she'd felt before. She felt like she was being watched. It was as if an unseen person was walking just behind her, studying her every move. Hillary gave in to her feelings once and turned quickly just as she was about to sit at Emily's desk. Of course, there was no one there.

There never had been anyone, she told herself, only half believing it. Or, if there was someone, he was a phantom, from her own imagination. And, as such, her phantom wasn't anyone she needed to worry about.

She switched on Emily's computer, scanning the main menu for the information she needed. Though she could certainly check them, she wasn't worried about the weather or crop reports. It was the payroll accounts that she felt might contain something of use. She keyed the payroll section and watched the spreadsheet fill the screen. Then it was merely a task of running through the files, looking for anything unusual in the money paid out to their workers.

What that unusual item might be, she didn't know. But someone had burned their files for a reason, and she couldn't just assume that the destruction of Albert's check registers was that reason. She'd have to look through everything that might possibly have been in those file cabinets.

A cold breeze flickered over her shoulders. It was as if someone had walked swiftly behind her, brushing the air aside as they moved. That impression was so complete that Hillary almost turned again, but she stopped herself. There was no one there, and she knew it.

The employee records, which had indeed been up-to-date on the computer, didn't seem irregular in any way. No one was earning drastically more or less than normal; no one had been fired or had quit without notice. In short, the company's relations with its employees were proceeding on an even keel. There was no evidence of a motive for murder.

She'd have been greatly surprised if there had been anything out of the ordinary. The de Gaetano winery paid the highest wages in the valley as a matter of course. Long ago, the family had established the practice of sharing the profits of good years with the employees, and the loyalty they enjoyed from their work force was legendary.

Outside the office window, dark clouds were slipping over the sun and occasional tendrils of lightning flickered at the tops of the western range of the Mayacamas. The breeze picked up slightly, as though threatening rain. There'd be no rain, though. The vineyards were helped by their position on the mountain slopes, but the drought that had afflicted all of California wasn't about to be broken just yet. No, like many nights, the clouds would only toy with the notion of relieving the dryness before breaking up and moving on.

Finishing with her search of the employee records, Hillary sat back and rubbed her eyes. She didn't really feel like doing this. What she wanted to do was sleep. *Rest and sleep.*

Hillary started in the chair, shaking her head against the sudden urge to sleep that had overcome her. It was only seven-fifteen, still light out. To be sleepy at this hour wasn't like her at all. She hadn't even had dinner yet.

Perhaps that was it. If she took time to eat, she might have the energy she'd need to continue with her tedious task. But no, she wasn't really hungry, either, and she didn't want to delay her search. With a new sense of resolve she left the spreadsheet program and keyed the field reports.

Nobody would commit murder over field reports, she told herself. Nonetheless, she began reading the material in the files. And, the more she read, the more sure she was that this particular avenue of her search was a dead end, too.

This year, the vineyards had suffered from drought, low moisture content and delayed growth: that was the sum of the information contained in those files. The harvest would be small, but it wouldn't be as bad for them as it was for some vineyards. They had always done business conservatively, and so had the financial stability to weather bad times. With careful management of the grapes and no waste, they'd be just fine. In fact, according to the reports, their pinot noir grapes were doing exceptionally well even with limited water. They might be headed toward a vintage year with the pinot noir.

Wine was usually only marked with the year of a particular vintage if the wine from that year was judged to be of exceptional quality. Almost all wine consisted of different grapes blended together to produce a consistent quality and taste. But sometimes the grapes matured in just the right manner to create a fine wine without tempering their taste with more mature wines from earlier pressings.

They'd never had a vintage year with their pinot noir. At least, none that they were satisfied to label as such. The pinot noir grape was temperamental and didn't do well in most American vineyards. Hillary's father had planted their first pinot noir vines when she was a child, putting in the first plants himself and caring for them like children. Those first grapes had done well enough to warrant planting an entire field in pinot noir. And, though they'd yet to achieve a truly world-class wine with them, they'd had several years of quite acceptable wine. Maybe this year would be their year.

That was the only high point contained in the file Hillary was reading. Everything else showed them heading toward an unexceptional year unless Franz could work a minor miracle in the fermenting vats. Hillary yawned. She still felt so tired.

She got up, stretched and walked to the window to watch the clouds overhead. Even if they burst forth with a deluge of rainfall, it was too late. Any water the grapes took on this close to harvest would just dilute their sugar content and lengthen the fermenting process.

Hillary rubbed her eyes and returned to the computer. She couldn't think off hand what else would have been in those file cabinets. How had so much time passed, she wondered vaguely. It was almost eight o'clock now, time for dinner.

Smiling wryly, she thought of another task that demanded her attention. She would have to go to town and give Jeff a small piece of her mind about his calling to warn Chief McDonald. She was no longer mad about it, but she didn't want him trying to protect her. Not like that.

They'd always had an open relationship based from the start on a feeling of equality between them. Occasionally, he'd shown his protective side. Once, when she was seven, he'd taken the blame for breaking a car window. He hadn't batted an eye when old man Foche came roaring toward them with Hillary's baseball in his hand, demanding to know who had cracked the passenger window of his Cadillac. Jeff had said he'd done it and that was that. Hillary kept her mouth shut, grateful to be spared the old man's wrath.

André Foche had been a nasty man by all accounts, and Hillary had known enough by that time to stay away from him. Quick-tempered and easily offended, André remembered all offenses against him and as often as not took the offenders to court.

But there was another reason Hillary had kept quiet that day. The Foches and the de Gaetanos had been on each other's bad sides since before her father was born. They were neighboring landowners; both families had come to the valley at about the same time. But instead of behaving in a neighborly manner, Charles Foche and his son, André, had taken every opportunity to squabble with the de Gaetanos. Most of their complaints centered around the land. In fact, the pinot noir vines were now planted on land that the Foches had always claimed was stolen from them years back. They had no proof of that claim, but that had never deterred them from pressing it.

On the day Hillary had broken André Foche's car window, the old man had been at their home complaining about land boundaries again. So when Jeff had claimed credit for the damage, she'd kept her mouth shut and let him accept the old man's wrath.

She'd been grateful then, extremely so. Jeff had only laughed and roughed up her hair, saying, "Don't throw so high next time. My arm won't stretch that far." And he'd said no more about it. Yes, she'd been grateful then. And, in a way, she was grateful now. But she wasn't seven years old anymore. She had to face up to life in her own way and he would have to realize that.

Thinking of Jeff, she switched off Emily's computer and started toward the door. A sudden break in the clouds sent a burst of sunlight across the valley just then, and the light flooding through the window helped cast a shadow on the floor in front of her. Hillary looked toward the window and saw the silhouette of a man's head on the other side of the glass. The clouds moved on. Jeff?

Yes, it was—no, it wasn't Jeff. And just as she took note of the black hat and the simple white collar and bolo tie around the man's neck, he disappeared.

Hillary froze in place, watching the window and waiting for any sound of intrusion. But she was alone, she thought. She felt eyes upon her again. She imagined that the man was just to her side and behind her...watching and waiting.

But waiting for what?

JEFF GOT NO ANSWER at Hillary's home and was about to call the winery when someone knocked.

"Yes?" he called. He replaced the phone receiver.

"Good afternoon, Jeffery." Bernard Foche stepped into Jeff's office brusquely, the English driving cap he habitually wore clutched in one bony hand. "Hell of a note about Albert, right? Quite a shock."

"Yes, quite a shock." Jeff spoke blankly as he watched the man enter and sit uninvited. "What can I do for you, Bernie?"

Because Bernard Foche hated to be called "Bernie," Jeff always used that familiar form when speaking to him. As the owners of the newspaper, the Simpson family had been on the receiving end of the Foche temper many times over the years. The newspaper had been sued six times by the family, which was six times more than any other resident of the Napa Valley. So, as with the de Gaetanos, the Simpsons and the Foches had no love lost between them.

A tall, thin man, Bernard Foche looked like a degenerate stork, Jeff thought. Bernard's dark hair was cut to a moderate length and combed back from his high hairline, leaving his facial features adrift in the middle of his wide, hard-jawed face. "I was wondering after Hillary," he finally said. "Haven't seen her yet," he continued. "How's she holding up?"

"You know Hillary," Jeff offered in as friendly a tone as he could muster. "She's tough. She'll make it."

"Good, good. It's hard to lose a family member. Damn hard."

Jeff watched as Bernard crossed his legs and placed his cap on his knee. The normally assertive man seemed unsure of himself.

"Is she at home, do you know?"

"No, I don't believe so. She didn't answer her phone."

"At the winery, then, do you think?"

"Probably. Why do you need to reach Hillary?"

"A business matter," Bernard answered quickly. "Nothing serious. And I don't want to bring it up, except that it's best to get these things out of the way right off, don't you think?"

"That depends on the business, I believe." Jeff didn't like the tone of Bernard's voice. It was insincere. But then the man had always had too short a fuse to wait for anything.

"Yes, well, my business can wait if she's not up to it," Bernard said now. He stood suddenly, a frown darkening his features. "She's at the winery?"

"So far as I know, she is." Jeff stood, too, on impulse. He felt nervous now, as though the other man had brought the feeling in with him and was endeavoring to leave it there.

"Yes, well, maybe I'll check." Bernard looked around the office, seemingly perplexed. There was an unfocused quality to his gaze. When he looked directly at Jeff again his normal belligerence returned. "I'll see you later," he said quickly. Then he turned and walked out of the room.

Jeff sat again, looking at the open doorway. What kind of business could Bernie Foche have with Hillary? She hadn't mentioned anything. He couldn't think of any circumstance where Hillary would involve herself in a business deal with Bernie. It was all too strange.

The man's manner was strange, too. He'd seemed almost disoriented at times. That wasn't like him. Not like him at all. It was as if he'd been reading from a script of some kind. Yes, he'd seemed like an actor doing his lines badly. Albert had seemed like that at times before his death, too. It was as though he hadn't really known what he was doing or why. But Albert hadn't been quite as distant and distracted as Bernie had been. Still, it was odd that two people would be acting so strangely.

He was about to call the winery for Hillary when his phone rang. Jeff scooped up the receiver and answered quickly, hoping it was Hillary. "Hello?"

Then he frowned. He picked up a pen to make a note on the pad on his desk. "You're sure about this?"

After listening for a moment, he said, "Okay. Yes, go ahead and follow up on that. Call as soon as you know anything. But don't talk to anyone but me. Right. Goodbye."

Jeff looked at his pad for a moment, then tore off the top sheet and strode purposefully from his office. He had to find Hillary.

HILLARY HAD WALKED around the entire winery building but had not been able to find signs of anyone having been there. There were no footprints or tire tracks. The winery was surrounded by the low vines of the vineyard; she could see no one running away from the building. The man couldn't simply disappear, could he?

Her head was pounding as she reentered the building. She wasn't insane; she wasn't seeing things. There had to have been someone out there. But where had he gone? Why was he there at all?

The only logical thing to do was to tell Jeff about her visions. She'd shied away from telling him before now, thinking it was a temporary effect of the shock of Albert's murder. She couldn't believe that now. No, she felt as fit as possible under the circumstances. She hadn't been drinking and was well rested. There was no reason for her to be seeing things. So she'd get Jeff's input. He was the only person she could rely on completely. And he was certainly the only one to whom she would willingly confide her growing fear.

For she was afraid. Deep inside, still small, the fear was growing. She had good cause for the fear. First of all, her cousin had been murdered. The killer was still at large and had burned their files in conjunction with his crime. That suggested premeditation. And she might not be able to deal with the killer alone. Secondly, she had seen a man who didn't seem real. She'd seen him three times and had felt his presence continually all day. Could someone be trying to drive her mad? It was possible, but if someone wanted her out of the way why hadn't the person just killed her as they had Albert? Perhaps that was the next move. Furthermore, though there might possibly be a human agent at work, one who was consciously trying to drive her insane, she couldn't imagine how the person could have made her dreams seem real. That was simply not possible.

And if it wasn't possible? Then she had seen a ghost. Actually, that was almost comforting. A ghost would pose less of a threat than a human killer. She didn't believe that a ghost could hurt her, but a human being certainly could.

"Get real," she said aloud. She forced a laugh as she returned to the desk for her purse. "There're no such things as ghosts."

The computer screen came to life across the room just as she spoke. Words scrolled rapidly up the screen, harsh black against the white of the monitor. Hillary froze. The computer had been off, and it wasn't connected to a modem that might allow remote use.

It was off. It couldn't be running.

The printer came to life, spitting out a line of words. Like a machine gun firing quickly, it fell silent when its objective had been accomplished. The paper rolled up with a discreet hum and stopped.

The computer screen suddenly became dark.

Even the birds outside seemed to fall silent then, as though waiting for Hillary to take her next breath. When she did breathe, she was filled with a sudden dizziness that threatened to bowl her over. The fear that had been lurking within her exploded, claiming total control of her limbs so that she couldn't move at all.

This can't be happening!

Taking a deep, calming breath, Hillary walked deliberately around the desk and to the printer. She could see two lines of print. She was just reaching for the paper when a voice stopped her.

"Hillary!"

She spun around, staring at the figure in the doorway.

"Awful dark in here, don't you think?" His arm moved to the side, groped for a second, and then found the switch. It was Bernard Foche.

"Bernie!" The word spilled out of her on a sigh of relief. She'd never been so glad to see her disagreeable neighbor in her life.

"Are you all right?" He moved into the office, regarding her blankly. "The door was open, so I stepped in. No lights on, of course, but your car is outside. Did I startle you?"

"Yes," she admitted. "Just a bit. I—I was about to go home." Hillary reclaimed control of her palpitating heart, managing to present a businesslike front.

"Sorry." Bernard smiled, coming closer.

"Yes, well, that's all right." Suddenly aware of how close he was to the page in the printer, Hillary stepped away from the message quickly, moving to pat Bernard's shoulder as she passed him. "The sun seems to have left me in the dark, didn't it?"

"Yes," he replied. He turned to watch her, and Hillary noted thankfully that he apparently hadn't noticed the page in the printer. She'd be damned if she was going to have him read the mysterious printout before she did.

"So, what brings you out here, Bernie?" Hillary spoke in a cheerful manner, regarding him openly.

"I wanted to convey my sympathy about Albert." Bernard spoke in an overly measured way, with an unreal tone. "I am very sorry, you know. I want you to know that if there's anything you need, you should feel free to call me."

"Thank you, Bernard." Hillary was touched by his sympathy because it seemed so hard for him to express it. "I appreciate your concern."

"Good, because I don't want you to feel shy about calling."

He held his cap nervously in his hands, his head craned forward on his long neck as though he was peering at something. His stance and the mechanical tone of his voice seemed odd. She accepted that he would feel uncomfortable expressing his sympathy to her after so many years of acrimony, but she couldn't believe that his discomfort would reduce him to this level of awkwardness. He was standing there like a grammar-school boy forced to confess to shoplifting.

"There's no need to feel shy, Bernard," she said. Something wasn't right with him. What was it? "Thank you. I'm finished here, now. Is there something else you wanted to say?" Hillary took her purse from the desk and walked toward the door.

"I—no—I guess not at the moment." Bernard smiled, slapped his cap against his leg and walked with her out of the office. Some of his normal manner seemed to be returning now, though he lacked his usual abruptness. "I'll leave you alone, dear." He nodded. "Good night."

"Good night, Bernard."

With a wave of his hand, he drove away. She watched his car move along the winding road through the vines. The scene was lit by the last drops of golden sunlight that spilled over the mountains to the west.

When he was out of sight, Hillary returned to the office. Her heart was thudding in her chest as she switched on the light.

She half feared the paper would be blank when she returned, as though leaving the office might have broken whatever spell she'd been under. But the printer was just as she'd left it, the words still on the page of continuous form paper extending beyond the platen.

Standing over the printer, Hillary read the sheet with a growing sense of unreality.

Old houses secret with decay. Old loves smile softly to betray. Old dreams, old fears, never die. And old lovers **will** never release the living nor abdicate the vigil of their love.

As she tore the sheet from the printer, the distinct sound of laughter filled the room.

Chapter Six

Jeff rushed up the winding road from town and toward the de Gaetano vineyards. The unsettled feeling he'd had lately now enveloped him. Bernard's visit and the phone call he'd received bothered him. The questionable circumstances surrounding Albert's death had become more unsettling with closer scrutiny, and Jeff had decided that it was time he got to Hillary with the latest news.

Following the road onto de Gaetano property, he took the left fork to the house first. He didn't even need to get out of his Jeep. Her car wasn't there, so he spun in a tight arc on the gravel drive and roared back to the winery. Yes, rounding the last curve through the vineyards, he saw her car. A light was on in the office. It was nearly nine o'clock, and she was still hard at work.

Jeff pulled to a stop beside her car and jumped out of his vehicle. "Hillary?" he called as he threw open the front door and hurried down the hall to the office. Just as he was about to enter, the door flew shut in his face.

"Hillary!" Jeff tried the knob. It was locked. "Hillary! Open up. It's me, Jeff!" He pounded on the door, his anxiety rising. "Hillary!"

What had happened? Why had she slammed the door in his face?

"Hill!"

He was about to throw himself at the door when it flew open. Hillary stood staring at him in surprise.

"What are you shouting about, Jeff?" She smiled. He looked frazzled, as though he'd expected to find something horrible behind the office door.

"The door was locked," Jeff said. "Are you all right?"

"I'm fine." She grasped his arm, leading him into the office. "The door wasn't locked, though."

"But the knob wouldn't turn." He let her lead him inside. "Didn't you close it?"

"Of course not," she said. She hadn't been looking when the door slammed shut. For that matter, she hadn't noticed that it was closed at all until she'd heard him pounding. She hadn't heard it close. In fact, she couldn't think of what she had been doing at the time. It was strange how things were slipping from her mind.

"Come on," she said to him. "I've got something to show you."

"What is it, Hill? Did you find something?"

"No, someone sent me something. At least, that appears to be what happened." She picked up the printout and handed it to her friend. "What do you think?"

Hillary watched as Jeff read the brief note, paying attention to the movement of his careful eyes on the page and the small smile that graced his lips when he'd finished.

"Bad poetry," he pronounced, smiling at her. "Whose?"

"I don't know. It came out of the computer."

"What, Emily wrote it?"

He didn't understand, and Hillary knew she was going to sound like a fool when she explained it. Still, this was Jeff she was talking to. He wouldn't think her foolish.

"No, the computer came on by itself and sent this out through the printer." Hillary shrugged, trying to seem unconcerned as she spoke, though the memory of the other events was pressing at her. "And there's no modem on this computer, so it wasn't sent in from outside," she added.

"Okay, the computer turned itself on and printed out a poem for you?" He looked again at the paper in his hand, then at Hillary. "Really?"

"Yes, really." Hillary smiled despite herself. It seemed rather silly once she'd said it out loud and not at all threatening. Still, it had happened.

"I don't know what to say about that, Hill." Jeff shrugged. "I imagine there's an explanation of some sort, though. Maybe Emily did write it and it printed out because of some glitch."

"I hope so," she said. "Though I doubt it."

Hillary was willing to hang on to Jeff's explanation, for the moment, anyway. But, given her other experiences, she didn't think there was a glitch. No, there was something else at work here.

Abruptly, Hillary took her purse and started toward the door. "Let's go to the house," she said. "I've got a lot of things to tell you." She would rather get more comfortable before she launched into her story, and she suddenly did not want to stay in the office, not when the computer seemed to be sending its own messages.

"I've got some news, too," Jeff said, following her. "Did Bernie Foche find you?"

"Yes, he did." Hillary switched off the lights, then she and Jeff walked outside. The summer evening was cool. "He was almost sweet."

"Really? I thought he was spooky when he came by the paper to ask about you." Jeff stood by his car. He watched Hillary get into hers as if unable to move until she'd closed her car door and obscured his complete view of her.

"Well, that too," Hillary said through the open window of her car. "I'll meet you at the house."

Hillary started her car and roared away from the winery. Jeff stood for another moment, watching her. He smiled. Always in a hurry, Hillary seemed forever to be roaring away from him. He wondered if that would ever change.

"I ALMOST FORGOT that I'm mad at you," Hillary said. She was standing in the doorway to her house as Jeff approached. She felt better here. In spite of the vision she'd had in the living room, this was her home and it held her warmest memories. She felt that those memories would keep her safe from whatever might be lurking outside.

"Mad at me? Why?" Confusion gave Jeff's rugged features a wary cast, and he regarded her through narrowed but friendly eyes.

"What did you tell Chief McDonald?" She tapped her forefinger against his chest when he reached her, a knowing smile gracing the regal lines of her face.

"McDonald?" Jeff grinned, his confusion dropping away. He grasped her hand and held it firmly. "Oh, I just told him that he'd better get out of your way once you get a head of steam up. Nothing else."

"You didn't call him to suggest that he might want to sideline me with busy work, did you? You know, keep me safe and all that?" Though she might have been angry with her friend, it was hard to remain so in his presence.

"No, actually, he was returning Gil Dickinson's call and I took it."

"And took the opportunity to ask him to keep me safe?"

"I wouldn't do that, Hillary. There'd be no point in trying to keep you out of something like this. I just mentioned your determination to keep up with developments."

"Well, he took it as a warning, I think," she said, allowing him to retain possession of her hand as she turned to go inside. The contact with his broad, strong hand was comforting and she was in no hurry to let go. "He didn't exactly get out of my way, as you suggested. I can't get into the house until tomorrow."

"That wasn't my suggestion," Jeff said, releasing her hand. "Though I'll have to admit I don't want to see you getting too far ahead of the police on this." He brought his hand up and clasped her shoulder. "I believe there was a crew from the state lab due in this afternoon, anyway. I don't suppose anyone went in but them."

"Okay, I suppose not." She led him to the kitchen where she began filling the coffeemaker on the counter. "But I don't see how they're going to find anything now. Half the force must have traipsed through the house last night."

"I would imagine they have their ways of looking past all of that. Gil is more up on that sort of thing than I am. He'd be the one to ask. Now, what did you want to tell me?"

"I don't know where to begin," she said, the thought of the poem flooding back into her mind. "Let's get comfortable first. It might take awhile, and I haven't eaten. You said that you had news?"

"Yes, but it can wait. I've got a feeling that I'll want to hear your information first."

"All right. But it's all pretty strange. Would you care for a ham sandwich?" She opened the fridge door and removed the ingredients for her meager supper. Suddenly, she was hungry enough to eat a seven-course meal, and her plans for a sandwich and coffee seemed far less than adequate.

"Sounds good." Jeff pulled a chair up to the table and opened a package of bread. "Now, if I have this straight, the computer came on and started writing poetry without provocation."

"Exactly." Hillary smiled down at him, knowing full well that it sounded crazy. "But there's more than that. I'd better start at the beginning, then you can tell me if I'm nuts."

"I can already tell you that you're not nuts, Hillary."

"That's kind of you, Jeff, but you'd better listen first."

Hillary began with the first strange dream she'd had in New York, outlining the sense of dread that had grown with each dream that followed. Speaking in a conversational tone while they ate, she tried hard not to draw any conclusions, letting him have the facts as she knew them and nothing more.

For the most part, he listened without comment. But when she mentioned the similarity between him and the man in her dream, he raised his eyebrows. He obviously thought what she'd already considered, that her external worries had prompted the dream and that she'd subconsciously peopled it with familiar faces.

But even if that were true, it couldn't explain her seeing the man here, in her home, as well as at the police station and the winery office. When she came to that part, Jeff could no longer keep quiet.

"You're sure that you saw someone?" he asked. "I mean, eyes open and wide awake?"

"Yes, Jeff, I'm sure." Hillary spoke calmly. It was a logical question, after all, and one that deserved full consideration. "I couldn't state unequivocally that I didn't nod off in McDonald's outer office, but I was awake here and at the winery. I was walking from the dining room to the living room when I saw him here."

"Okay, I'll buy it. But don't ask me to explain it."

Unfortunately, an explanation was exactly what she wanted, and she filled his coffee cup without saying anything, letting him have a moment to think. "So, am I crazy?" she asked, at last.

Jeff looked at her seriously, letting his calm blue eyes follow their own direction over her face. Hillary wondered what he was thinking as he regarded her. His gaze seemed so intent upon her face, it was as though he expected some outward flaw to give evidence of her insanity. To Hillary's immense relief, he smiled and reached for her hands.

"You are the most sane person I know," he said. "Given the shock that you've been through since you've been back, I think it's logical enough that you might suffer some ill effects.''

''Which is a fairly fancy way of saying I'm nuts,'' she pointed out, but not without humor.

''In shock, maybe,'' Jeff stated, earnestly. He squeezed her hand. ''Look at it logically. You had some dreams that you took as warnings, and—''

''I never said they were warnings,'' Hillary cut in.

''They prompted you to come back here, even though Albert assured you that everything was just fine. Right?''

''Right,'' she admitted.

''And what happened almost as soon as you got off the plane? There was a fire at the winery and your cousin was murdered. It seems like your premonitions were right on the money, Hillary.'' Jeff nodded, thinking it through even as he spoke.

''Which still doesn't explain these...*hallucinations.*'' Hillary sipped her coffee, feeling vaguely that, logical though it might seem, he was missing the mark.

''I don't really know what caused them,'' he admitted. ''But this dream man warned you, and he was right. So, I'd guess that he's about the most reliable fellow you could have to turn to right now. It would seem logical that you would bring him out in the open somehow, where he can do more good.''

''Oh, baloney,'' Hillary scoffed, laughing. ''So you figure I've manufactured some knight in shining armor to protect me from the cold cruel world? Give me some credit, Jeffery.''

''Not consciously,'' Jeff said, quickly. ''But Albert's murder was a big shock. You're damn good at handling life on your own, but how can anyone cope with such a shock on their own? Nobody can.''

"But I've got you," she said.

"Yes and you always will," he said with soft sincerity. "But it's not as though we're in constant contact. We're usually three thousand miles apart, and you're on your own every day. Anyway, I think you did generate the dream man."

"How many psychology classes did you take at college, Jeff?" she chided him. "I thought your major was business."

"I'm just making it all up," he admitted. "But I think it makes sense. Maybe not enough sense, but some." And he wished it didn't. He also wished she felt close enough to call on him no matter how many miles might separate them, but, unfortunately, she didn't. That simple fact seemed sadder than Albert's death at the moment.

"All right, it makes some sense." Hillary noted the sadness that slipped into her friend's eyes and wondered why he was suddenly so down. She was reluctant to ask. "So, now that I've had it all explained, my dream man should go away. Right?"

"Just like magic," he said.

Jeff smiled, but it seemed forced to Hillary. "And what about the poem?"

"A glitch in the system," he said. It sounded more like a question than a firm reply. "I really don't know."

"And what about the fire? I distinctly heard someone say 'fire' when I was in my living room. And when I went to the winery, there was indeed a fire. How did that happen?"

"I wouldn't rule out ESP," he said, shrugging.

"ESP? Come now, I've never shown any sign of that before. I don't expect to start now."

"Hey, considering ESP is studied seriously in universities, then it's possible that it's happened to you. It might explain the dreams as well."

"But, if my dreams were some kind of prescient experience, that would seem to rule out your explanation of my seeing the man here."

"Don't try to pin me down on this stuff, Hill!" Jeff laughed heartily, breaking the melancholy that had come over him moments before. "I'm just guessing."

"Yes, well, I think we're both nuts," she said, laughing in return. "This whole conversation is nuts, for that matter. It's probably all just jet lag. A good night's sleep will put everything back in place."

"That's right. But I hope my diagnosis has helped you."

"Sure, it's helped me realize that I can rely on you." She patted his hand, and then stood to get the carafe of coffee. "Of course, we're still stuck with the question of who killed Albert and why."

"Yes, exactly." Jeff sipped at the steaming liquid after Hillary filled his cup. "I was coming to see you about that tonight. How much business do you do in San Francisco?"

"Our distributor is there," she said. "Some suppliers. That's about all."

"What about banking?"

"Here in town, of course. But I handle the majority of our funds in New York. Why?" His interest in de Gaetano business threw her off. What could he have found out about their business that would concern Albert's murder?

"You said that Albert had been making a lot of trips to the city for the last few months."

"Yes, but they probably weren't business-related."

"So you don't have any money in Golden Gate Fidelity?"

"No. What are you getting at?" Hillary found his reporter's habit of keeping his own information close to his vest while pumping an interview subject annoying at the moment, and she wished he'd get to the point.

"I think Albert has an account there," he said, pursing his lips in thought.

"Why?"

"Because I— Oh, I'm sorry. I'm ahead of myself on this, Hillary. You don't know about the detective."

"Detective? What detective?"

"A guy named Lemuel Chambers in San Francisco," Jeff said. "He did some work on a story for the paper last year. I called him in to do some checking."

"What? Why didn't you tell me?" Hillary didn't like to be in the dark about developments in her own life, and it bothered her that he'd gone ahead with something like this without informing her. "When did you do this?"

"Just this morning, Hillary," Jeff said quickly. "I'm running a paper, and I've got to check it out, anyway. We used Lemuel last year because it was quicker and cheaper than having Gil or me go down to San Francisco and pay for a hotel room."

"Yes, but why did you hire him now?"

"To find out what Albert was doing in San Francisco," Jeff said innocently. "It'll speed things up."

"I see," Hillary said, smiling again. "I keep forgetting that you're a reporter first and foremost. But really, you didn't have to save the news as some kind of scoop."

"Sorry, but I didn't feel like saying anything until I had some news. Besides, you'd have wanted to pay his fee if I had told you, and I didn't want that."

"Okay." She laughed. "But how did he find out about the bank?" Hillary yawned, beginning to feel the effects of the past couple of days.

"I faxed Lemuel a photograph of Albert, and he's been showing it to cab drivers at the airport," Jeff said. "So far, he's found three drivers who remember Albert. Two of them have taken him to that bank."

"Where did the third take him?"

"The ballpark."

"Ballpark?" Hillary blinked away the fatigue that was beginning to drag at her limbs. "That's not very sinister."

"No, but it helps establish his destinations in San Francisco. Lemuel's going to keep at it with the taxis again tomorrow. I told him not to try getting anything from the bank. As Albert's next of kin, you'll have to check on that."

"Yes, I suppose so." The coffee, even as strong as she'd made it, wasn't doing anything to keep her awake, and she yawned again.

"Tired?" Jeff finished his coffee. "Maybe we'd better call it a night."

"Yes, I think so." Hillary stood, beginning to clear away the plates and cups. No, she could do that in the morning. All she wanted to do now was sleep. "I don't understand why I'm so tired."

"It is after midnight." Jeff stood with her, surprised at how late it had gotten. "Will you be all right tonight?"

"Oh yes, I'll be just fine." Hillary slipped her arms around him, hugging him briefly. "You've been so much help already, Jeff. Thank you."

"It wasn't any trouble." He returned her embrace, kissing her cheek. "You get a good night's sleep. We'll go over to Albert's in the morning. Maybe we'll have more news from San Francisco, too."

"Maybe." Looking at Jeff after she'd stood back from him, Hillary was struck by an urge to renew the embrace. All his years of friendship were evident in the heartfelt tone of his voice and the sober reflection in his eyes. He was too good for her, she thought. And she felt eternally grateful that he apparently didn't share that opinion. "You get some sleep, too," she said. "I'm not the only one up past bedtime."

"I'll do that." He stroked her cheek, a frown darting over his face for a moment. He kissed her once more, briefly, on the lips. Smiling now, he stepped toward the door. "Good night, Hillary."

"Good night."

Hillary stood for a moment looking at the empty place he'd occupied in the kitchen door. His kiss had provoked a new feeling within her, touching an emotion well beyond the friendship she'd always felt for the man. After so many kisses exchanged in greeting or parting, none had resonated as deeply as that simple, shy kiss. It had made her want another kiss, and another. As she contemplated that feeling, it grew into something akin to need.

But that was probably logical, wasn't it? He was her last link to everything now. Her friend, confidant and protector, Jeff Simpson was all she had now, so of course she'd feel something for him. When she recovered from the shock of the past days she'd feel differently about him. There was no use imagining that their relationship was going to become romantic.

Still, it felt good to think about Jeff. It was a warm feeling, both urgent and peaceful at the same time, and she didn't want to lose it. Loving Jeff Simpson wouldn't be the worst thing in the world, would it?

No, it wouldn't. But letting her tattered emotions get the better of her might be terrible, especially if she were to act on grief-induced feelings. Nothing could destroy a friendship faster than trying to force it into something more. Of course she loved Jeff, as he loved her, but the love of a friend was entirely different. And she valued his friendship far too much to lose it.

Hillary staggered slightly, suddenly aware that she'd begun to fall asleep standing in the kitchen. Smiling wryly, she switched off the coffeemaker and walked to her bedroom, turning out the lights as she went. She was so tired that she wasn't entirely sure if she could manage to disrobe before giving in to sleep.

Tired. So tired.

She slipped beneath the sheets in her underclothes, consciousness dropping away as her head hit the pillow.

"Yes, dear," her dream man said. "You're tired. You've had a terrible time of it, and you must rest now."

"But there's so much to do," she mumbled, shifting in her sleep.

"Tomorrow," he told her. "There is time tomorrow."

"Will you be there?" Her words slipped below hearing, her lips unmoving.

"I'm always there, Marie. It wasn't I who left."

Hillary felt his hand smoothing her hair back from her face as she lay in the grass in the shade of the majestic old oak.

She could feel his breath moving quickly on the side of her face. He was nervous, she thought. No, embarrassed. Yes, embarrassed by her half-clothed state and unsure of how to react to it. Poor, sweet man. He was so provincial, so courtly in his manner toward her. He was fighting to remain a gentleman.

"I'm tired," she said.

"Yes, and you must sleep." He took his hand away. And she could feel that he was restraining himself from kissing her. "I'll write another poem for you," he told her.

"That would be nice."

Something was wrong. She wasn't sure what it was. She was too tired to reason through it, but something was wrong.

"When we're together again I will write poems for you every day. And I won't let anyone harm you again. Never again."

"But I'm not harmed," she began.

"Don't talk. Sleep. We'll talk again at a later time."

No, this was not right. She was in her bedroom, wasn't she? She wasn't outside on a lazy summer day. She wasn't here with . . . with whom?

Hillary turned onto her back, looking up at him. Jeff? No, his face was thinner, his Adam's apple more prominent. It wasn't Jeff.

"Who are you?" She began to rouse herself, fighting to regain consciousness. "Where am I?"

"Quiet, my love," he said. "I'll let you sleep."

That reassurance was enough to calm her fears. He wouldn't harm her, she knew that now. He would never harm her; he loved her too much to do her harm.

"But I don't know you," she said, drifting off again.

"You will, dearest one. You will." And he turned his face away from her to conceal his tears.

HILLARY LAY IN THE MEADOW long after he had gone. The summer breeze was gentle and warm, caressing her tired limbs and rejuvenating them. She'd never had a dream that felt so perfect before, never lived anything so perfect. She didn't want to leave this place.

She didn't want to leave him. He was such a sweet, gentle man. She couldn't understand why she'd ever been afraid of him. It was foolish.

All he wanted to do was to love her. Surely there was no harm in that.

JUST AFTER THE MAN LEFT Hillary, Bernard Foche awoke from a fitful sleep. Only partially awake, he looked around his room as though expecting someone to be there. Had he heard something? No, nothing. Moments later, he was asleep again.

The man appeared slowly at the foot of his bed, and there was nothing benign or friendly about him now. His lips were twisted in an animal snarl, his sensitive fingers were curled into lethal fists as though he was about to pummel the sleeping man.

But he made no move to harm him, as his lips curled into a cruel smile.

"I've got you now," he said. "Murderer!"

Bernard awoke with a start, sitting upright and staring fearfully at the foot of his bed. He was staring at nothing. The man wasn't there.

Chapter Seven

The clouds cleared away, revealing the diamond-bright light of the stars overhead. They seemed to look down upon the valley. The night breezes freshened, rippling through the leaves of the vines and whispering through the slumbering town. The stars watched impassively, as they had since long before the grape had first come to the valley, overseeing the many small dramas played out amid the vineyards and pressing sheds that awaited another harvest of the earth's sweet nectar.

The stars had time to wait and watch. They had eternity. Those below them weren't so lucky. For some of them, their time might be numbered in only days.

These thoughts slipped through Hillary's half-sleeping mind and were lost. A distant ringing seemed to push them away. It sounded like a doorbell. Yes, that's what it was. But it didn't matter. Her callers could come back later if they wished. For now, Hillary wasn't willing to be disturbed.

She rolled slightly at the sound but didn't fully awaken. It had become full night on the hill beneath the tree, and the stars were out. They were majestically bright. Somewhere below a few kerosene lanterns shone. The light of the stars seemed miraculous to Hillary, so beautiful that she could just lie here, looking up at them forever.

Forever. Just as the stars had been looking down forever, she could return their kindly gaze for an equally long time.

The ringing sounded again. A strange, anachronistic sound, the ringing didn't belong here. There was no building nearby to be the source of the sound. No sign of humanity save the ordered vines below the hill. Where could that ringing be coming from?

Again she heard the bell. A pounding sound drifted in from far away. People should have more consideration than to ruin the beautiful evening with such a racket.

Reluctantly, Hillary sat, listening for the source of the sound. She could see nothing, but she rose to investigate.

She awoke abruptly when she stubbed her toe against the leg of a bureau near her bedroom door.

Sunlight flooded the room! She forced her eyes shut until she could adjust to the glare. What on earth? She hopped back to sit on her bed and massage the injured toe.

The doorbell rang; someone was leaning on the bell to prolong the jarring sound. And then came the pounding. "Hillary!"

"Yes! Just a minute!" Still groggy, Hillary found her robe and slipped into it as she hobbled to the front door. "I'm coming!"

"Are you all right?" Jeff burst through the door when she opened it, his sturdy face tight with worry. "I was about to break down the door."

"I'm fine," she said, closing the door. "Except that I just stubbed my toe. Come in." She yawned, rubbing her eyes with her fist.

"Ouch." Jeff winced in sympathy. "I didn't mean to rush you, but I feared the worst when you didn't answer."

"I must have been more tired than I thought." Leading him to the kitchen, she filled a cup with cold coffee and placed it into the microwave to heat. "Coffee?"

"No, I just had coffee with Gil."

"What time is it?" Hillary was beginning to come around now, but it was taking her an unusually long time to wake up.

"Ten o'clock." Jeff sat, studying her closely.

"That late? My goodness, why didn't you call me?"

"I expected you to come to town when you were ready, so I figured I'd wait. But when you didn't answer your phone and Emily told me that you hadn't gone to the winery, I got worried. You must have been out cold."

"Yes, but I think I slept too long." Arching her back slightly, she took her cup of hot coffee to the table and sat. "I'm all stiff."

"Ten hours or so of sleep should put you on track, though," he commented. He was still watching her as though he expected her to disappear at any moment.

"I had a dream, too," she said slowly. "But I'll be darned if I can remember what it was about."

"The man again?"

"I don't think so." Hillary caught only fragile fragments of her dream now, feelings really, nothing that could be described. All she could remember clearly was a feeling of contentment and peace, and that wasn't enough to bother telling Jeff about. "No," she said now. "Not the man. It was a nice dream, though. Pleasant."

"Good." Jeff smiled, noticing the smile that came over her face as she thought of the dream. "So, do you want to go through Albert's house? The police are done there."

"Yes, certainly." Hillary sipped at her coffee and then stood. "I'll be ready in ten minutes."

"No rush," Jeff called as she strode from the room. "And watch out for your toes."

Jeff sat very still for a moment, just listening to the diminishing sound of her movements in the house. The sound of her shower running broke his reverie, and he stood and took a cup from the cupboard and filled it with coffee. While the microwave heated his drink, he walked to the kitchen door and looked through to the living room.

Why did she feel the need to manufacture a protector when he was close at hand? Unfair as it was, the question bothered him. All their years of friendship had seemed to come to nothing in this crisis. Of course, it wasn't fair to hold her subconscious thoughts against her. And he wasn't bothered by feelings of not being appreciated; he knew that she needed him. No, what bothered him was the very nature of the dreams and projections she'd described to him. No matter how she might feel up front, in the deep core of her mind, Hillary didn't feel that she could depend on him. Or, worse yet, she didn't *want* to depend on him. And he wanted that so badly.

He couldn't have said when his feelings for her had deepened, but they had. He loved her gentle voice and the soft light of her eyes, loved her quick intellect and the joyous abandon of her laughter. Ironically, the very independence that haunted him now was another of the attributes that he loved.

Jeff had gotten to the point where he wasn't sure he could continue with their friendship, not if it wasn't able to grow into something more. It scared him to think of losing her as a friend, but he was equally fearful of not telling her how he felt. At the moment, he felt more lonely than he'd ever felt in his life.

He wanted to be as important to her as she was to him, but he wasn't. And it bothered him that she would look so much more content over the memory of a dream than she had when she had seen him. It was a lonely world, he thought, when you're not important to someone.

A GRASSY HILL. OAK LEAVES rustling in the warm breeze. Acres of grapevines, their fruit heavy from a plenitude of rain. The valley was perfect beneath the clear blue sky. Perfect.

Hillary shook her head, opening her eyes again and dipping her head beneath the hard spray of the shower. She'd nearly fallen asleep in the shower. It was as if the dream was so hypnotically beautiful that she couldn't wait to return to it.

"Snap to it, girl," she told herself, rinsing the soap away from her lithe, athletic body. She turned off the shower and threw open the door. Activity was what she needed, useful activity.

Toweling herself dry, she tried to remember the dream. It was as elusive as a harbor fog burning off in the morning light and she couldn't capture it. All she knew was that it was peaceful. And, though she didn't remember it, she felt certain now that the man had been in it.

What struck her most about her phantom visitor was how much he looked like Jeffery. Why had she given him her friend's face?

Did her feelings about Jeff's kiss last night have anything to do with that? Regarding herself in the mirror, she wondered what Jeff thought of her. Did he find her the least bit appealing? Beautiful, perhaps? Sometimes it seemed that he was looking at her with exactly those thoughts. Sometimes she had thoughts about him, as well.

She'd heard the arguments over the years that a man and a woman couldn't be friends without sexual feelings disrupting the relationship. Until now, she'd felt that she and Jeff would be an exception to that rule. Now, she wasn't sure. After all, there must be some reason that neither of them had married. Neither of them had been celibate over the years, but somehow, their friendship had seemed more important than their other relationships. It was as though they'd already found the companionship that marriage could offer. The only thing they'd lacked was sex.

She'd never looked at her body in a mirror as she did now. She'd never tried to fathom the male reaction to herself. Was she beautiful? She worked at being slim, and while there certainly were things she'd change about herself, she didn't find her body disagreeable overall. But was she beautiful? Would Jeff think she was beautiful if he were to see her right now?

The thought made her blush; she finished drying herself. There was no time for such wasteful speculations. Later, when she had time to sort out her own feelings, she could speculate. So, like writing an appointment into her calendar, she resolved to work this question out later.

When there was time.

BERNARD FOCHE STOOD outside the old house and regarded the sagging porch and the broken windows. He should tear the place down. It was an eyesore and a firetrap. More importantly, it might bring him a lawsuit if some kid were to be harmed in there. He should tear it down.

But no, if he tore it down, a workman might find...find what? He couldn't remember. All he knew was that the house had to remain intact for the time being. Later, he could have it demolished. Next year. Yes, he'd see to it next year.

When there was time.

ALBERT'S HOUSE had obviously suffered a benign but untidy invasion since they'd been there last. Everything was slightly out of place, just enough to make it feel wrong somehow, and there was residue from the pale blue fingerprint powder on many of the doorknobs and various surfaces throughout the house. In the kitchen, the flour and sugar containers had been searched and the pots and pans were stacked on the kitchen table.

Albert's bedroom showed the same signs of foreign occupation. His drawers were open, the clothing inside was rumpled, and his personal papers were arranged on the bed.

"They did a very complete job," Hillary commented blankly. Necessary as it all was, she found this invasion of her cousin's privacy to be horribly insulting. If he'd died of natural causes there'd have been no need of this. But then that wasn't the case, was it? "Do you suppose there's really anything for me to find here?"

"Nothing obvious, but if you dig a bit you'll probably find something." Jeff stood unhappily in the door of Albert's room. He didn't like doing this and didn't like subjecting Hillary to it, either. Right now he wished she were a bit less self-reliant and more willing to let the police do their work.

"We'd better go to his office, then." Hillary pushed aside some of the papers on the bed, revealing a small pile of torn cards. "Lotto tickets," she said. "A bunch of them."

"So Albert was bitten by the lotto bug, too." Jeff entered the room, smiling. "Did he win?"

"Doesn't look that way," she commented, scooping up the tickets. They were all torn in half...losers. "I wonder why he kept them."

"Probably to remind himself not to bother buying any more," Jeff offered, standing at her side. "I buy one ticket every New Year, myself."

Hillary felt buoyed by Jeff's presence at her side. She picked up another narrow slip. "Horse racing," she commented. Then she gave him the slip.

"You knew that he went to the track every now and again." But he expressed his interest with a short whistle after he read the ticket. "Five hundred dollars?"

"That's a pretty sizable bet for Albert."

"Damn right. He never went higher than five dollars any time I was with him."

"When was the last time you went to the track with Albert?"

"Oh, I don't know, I suppose it was two years ago now. Quite a while, anyway. Are there any other tickets?"

"No, just the one," she said. "Maybe he had a hot tip."

"Albert didn't believe in hot tips."

No, Hillary thought, he didn't. And he didn't buy lottery tickets, either. At least, she hadn't thought he did.

"Come on," Hillary said. "Let's get this over with." Dropping the lotto tickets, she turned abruptly and strode across the hall to the office.

It stank of stale wine inside and broken glass still crunched underfoot, though the bottle and much of the glass had been cleaned away. The couch had been covered by a white sheet, as though some thoughtful officer had known she would be coming and sought to spare her the sight of the blood. The glass and bottle that had been on the desk were gone, but it appeared that everything else was still there. Fingerprint powder dusted everything from the desktop to the windowsills and bookcases. Albert's gun case was on a low coffee table, blue powder coating it.

"I should check his drawers first, I suppose." Hillary sat in his chair, opened the middle drawer and began to gingerly sort through the contents.

"I'll start on the file cabinets, if you don't mind," Jeff said.

"Yes, please. I can't think of any winery business so shady that I'd be embarrassed if it showed up in the paper."

"Now, Hillary, I—" Jeff began, defensively.

"I'm just kidding," she said quickly. "When did you get so thin-skinned?"

"'Sorry, it feels a bit creepy here, that's all.'' He opened the top file, frowning at how he'd reacted to her joke. Her every remark seemed so personal now.

Hillary continued with her search of the drawers, but found nothing out of the ordinary. Her mind was wandering. Jeff was acting strangely lately. He was looking at her differently, and he seemed to be guarding his words very closely. Now this reaction. It was completely out of character for him.

Finishing the middle drawer with no success, Hillary opened the top drawer to her right and peered inside. The drawer was nearly empty, with only a few sheets of blank typing paper lying in the bottom. The next drawer was the same, containing only a couple paperback books and an unopened bill from the cable television company. The bottom drawer, of course, had contained the gun case. Now it held only a bottle of gun oil, a rag and a box of .38 caliber bullets.

Hillary took the box out of the drawer and opened it. There were a few bullets gone from the box, but not many. She angled the box and shook the bullets into line with each other. As near as she could tell, there weren't more than six missing. Just enough to have filled the chambers of his revolver once.

Hillary replaced the box of bullets and opened the top left-hand drawer. Empty again, totally empty.

"There isn't anything in these drawers," she said, turning the chair to look at Jeff. "Did the police take anything?"

"They would have told you if they'd taken anything from a drawer." He slipped the file he'd been looking at back into the file drawer and slid it shut, opening the next one. "Are there any particular areas you might expect to interest a burglar?"

"Areas of business? Why, no, not here. Anything he had here would have concerned the financial status of the company, not future plans as such. Everybody in the business knows all too well what the status of most wineries is these days. The drought is choking them off."

"Not you."

"No, and not the wineries owned by major liquor concerns or conglomerates, either. Many of us have a cash buffer to get us through tough times. But the independents are in a bind. There's no news in that."

"What if someone hoped to pull a takeover? Mightn't there have been something here to help them?" He continued thumbing through the files as he spoke. He didn't find anything of interest until he was midway through the drawer. He pulled out a file.

"We're not a public company, Jeff," Hillary was saying. "They couldn't just take us over."

"So there'd be no motive for robbery."

"I can't see where they'd gain anything here. I mean, whatever leverage they might hold against the winery could easily be countered in New York. We've built up a fairly substantial portfolio."

Jeff's gaze moved toward the window and out over the neighboring houses to the fields beyond. Then, frowning, he brought the file he'd pulled to the desk and laid it in front of Hillary.

"So, why are you borrowing money from Bernie Foche?"

"What?" The question came out of the blue; it was like a slap in the face. The very idea of borrowing money from Bernard Foche was horrid. "We don't…"

But the papers within the file folder belied the words she was about to say. It was a standard loan agreement form, signed and dated by both Albert and Bernard Foche. The paper stated the sum of money and the terms of its repayment.

"My, God," she whispered.

"You didn't know about that?" Jeff stood at her side, one hand on her shoulder.

"No, I didn't. And, had I known, I surely wouldn't have agreed with it. My goodness, Albert borrowed over two-hundred thousand dollars from Bernie!"

"Why? You said you weren't strapped for cash."

"We aren't." She turned the paper over, searching for what had been offered as collateral. Yes, there it was. "Damn him!" she exclaimed, slapping the paper down on the desk. "This is insane! Damn that whole family!"

"Why? What is it?"

"He made Albert put up the pinot noir as collateral!" Hillary was so angry that she had to stand to dissipate the sudden rush of energy that hit her. She paced between the desk and the window by the files. "Not just the land, Jeff. The vines as well. That weasel is trying to get the whole thing! And it's all due tomorrow!"

"So pay him back."

"With interest it's nearly two-hundred-sixty thousand dollars, Jeff. By tomorrow!"

"You said that you were in good shape."

"Yes, but raising cash that fast would involve selling massive chunks of our holdings. There'd be no time to maximize the profit, no time to maintain any order in the selling. And we'd be in poor shape if the drought continues and we needed to pump more cash into the winery."

"So we'll talk to Bernie. We'll extend the loan."

"I'm not asking him for anything! Not a minute of time!" Hillary was adamant. Her regal cheeks flushed with anger as she turned toward Jeff. "I'd sooner turn over the land and poison the vines. My father planted those vines himself, Jeff."

"You're not obligated to adhere to the terms of the loan if you didn't know about it, Hill," Jeff pointed out. "You didn't sign the papers, after all."

"I didn't have to. Albert ran the winery."

Hillary dropped back into the chair, her anger replaced by a sudden tired feeling of defeat. No, it wasn't the end of the world, but the thought of losing that land to Bernie was anathema to her. She would have to call New York and start selling stock.

"Why didn't Bernie tell you yesterday?" Jeff stood behind her, brushing her hair back slightly and massaging her shoulders with the slow, loving pressure of his capable hands. "He should have offered to extend it himself."

"He didn't mention it because he knew I wouldn't ask for an extension, and he wants the land. That's why."

The feeling of Jeff's hands on her tired shoulders was soothing, almost enough to calm her down. He was so kind to her, but he didn't understand. His family had, after all, won their battles with the Foches while the de Gaetano family had never obtained a satisfactory conclusion to the wrangling over the disputed land boundaries. The fight had gone on for three generations, and it looked like the current disputant had come closer than any in the past to actually getting the land. Well, he wouldn't get it. No matter what, he wasn't going to get their land.

"Let's see Bernie," she said. "I'm going to find out about this loan."

"Maybe you should check at the office first," Jeff suggested. "See if there's any mention of where Albert spent the money." He hated to see her in this state, and wanted to give her some time to calm down before seeing the other grower.

"Right. And we haven't found any check registers here, yet, either. Let's finish looking and then get to the winery."

They searched quickly and methodically, but found nothing. While they worked side by side, Hillary found herself wishing she could just quit for the day and find someplace peaceful to rest. Jeff was right, after all. Bernie couldn't hold her to the time limits of the loan in light of what had happened. She hadn't signed the agreement and could surely take him to court on the matter of collateral.

But using the legal system to get out of an obligation was a Foche tactic, and she wouldn't stoop to it. As much as she wanted to turn the mess over to someone else, she couldn't. She'd have to see it through to the end.

An hour after finding the loan paper, they were through. And, other than the information about the loan, they knew precious little more about Albert's death than they had when they'd begun. It had been a dispiriting morning's work, and Hillary got into Jeff's car in silence.

Looking back at the blank windows of Albert's house, she thought, for a brief moment, that she saw a movement inside her late cousin's room. It was a white blur, like a face at the window, and then nothing. It was probably just a shadow or her overactive mind. She looked away from the window pointedly, resolving not to let her imagination get the upper hand again.

There was no one at the window.

HE WALKED THROUGH Albert's room paying close attention to the items that Hillary and Jeff had examined. Lottery tickets and horse betting slips. Those were trash. What mattered was the paper that they had taken away with them. That was the key to Foche's downfall. By his own hand he would fall, brought down in the manner his elders had deserved.

Victory would be sweet. The great grandson of the murderer would be brought down as a murderer and suffer the tortures his family had escaped for all too long. He would pay for all of them. Pay with his life.

Watching the car pull out of the driveway and down the street, he allowed himself to smile. She was beautiful still. Timelessly beautiful. Hopelessly close now. He could barely restrain himself from grasping her to him right away. She would love him as dearly as he loved her once she knew him and knew how long he'd waited to have her returned to him.

But he had to wait until Bernard Foche was found out. He had to wait still longer. But he could afford to wait a bit. He had time.

He had nothing but time.

Chapter Eight

"I didn't know what to tell them, Hillary!" Emily's exclamation greeted Hillary and Jeff. "They had a warrant, after all. I couldn't stop them!"

"Wait! Start at the top, Emily. Who had a warrant?" Hillary asked. She glanced around the winery office.

"The police. They took our books."

"Why?"

"Taxes." All of the woman's feelings of fear were clear in the one word. "They think we're cheating," she elaborated.

"We're not, are we?"

"Hillary!" Emily looked at Hillary as though she had just asked if she had killed Albert. The denial was clearly evident in her voice and Emily didn't answer further.

"Okay," Hillary said calmly. "Then we've got nothing to worry about."

"But what if we're in violation of something and didn't know it?"

"Then we'll pay the fine and be done with it. Don't worry about it, dear," she said, patting the older woman's arm. "It will be fine."

"I tried to reach you," Emily continued, shaking her head in worry. "You must have gone already." She paused. "Here—here's the warrant."

Emily handed the folded paper to Hillary as though it might be booby-trapped and then sat at her desk with a relieved sigh.

"Is this all legal?" Hillary gave the document to Jeff, a look of tired resignation marring her face.

"Looks like it to me." Jeff had been more shocked than Hillary at this turn of events. Knowing the de Gaetanos as he did, he knew that they would sooner cut off a finger than cheat on their taxes. Besides, neither Hillary nor Albert was dumb enough to believe they could get away with tax evasion for very long. "Yes, it calls for all your records from the last three years. Boy, when you have a premonition, you don't mess around."

"No, I guess not." Hillary couldn't help but laugh. So far, everything that could go wrong had gone wrong. There didn't seem to have been much point in getting out of bed today. "I guess we don't have anything to look at here, then, do we?"

"Nothing on computer?" Jeff offered.

"I looked last night and didn't see anything unusual. Really, it's the books the police took that might actually be helpful. Emily," she said, turning to the other woman, "did we still have what they wanted? We didn't lose it in the fire?"

"No, we had most of it. I'm afraid that what we lost in the fire would have been the bills and charge slips to back up the tax statements."

"Oh, wonderful," Hillary said sarcastically. "Well, that's it, then. We're done here for today. You go on home, Emily. I'll call you in the morning."

"Are you sure?"

"Yes, go ahead." Hillary looked around the room feeling somewhat helpless.

"Well, I was ready for lunch, anyway," Emily said reluctantly. "But only if you're sure you'll be all right without me."

"I'm fine," Hillary reassured her. "I'd rather not do any business until we know more about the audit, anyway."

"I'll be at home if you need me." Emily took her purse from her desk and walked to the door. "Take it easy, Hillary. You don't look well."

"I will. Goodbye."

Hillary stared vacantly at the far wall without saying anything for a moment. Only after she heard Emily's car start outside did she look at Jeff. She smiled wanly. "You're awfully quiet," she said. "Thinking deep thoughts?"

"No, I'm feeling quite blank at the moment," he said. He came over to her and sat on the edge of the desk by her side. "The plot thickens, I guess."

"Boy, I guess so." Hillary shrugged. It was an uncharacteristic gesture of defeat.

"I wonder what set them off? It couldn't have been anything the police found yesterday."

"They took something from his drawers," she said.

"Yes, but they couldn't have gotten a warrant for financial records this fast."

"Which only makes it worse," Hillary pointed out. "Because that would mean that they've been investigating us for some time."

"Not so terribly long. Just long enough to find probable cause for a warrant. You know, I did think of one positive thing about this," he said. "They'll probably freeze your assets until they're done monkeying with your books."

"That's positive?"

"It is if you want to stall Bernie on that loan."

"You're right," she said, though his optimistic view of the matter didn't gain much ground against her somber mood. "I still won't be able to raise the money easily, but at least I can start setting up some deals."

"And you can find out what the money Albert borrowed was for, too. That might help."

"If I can at least stall Bernie until we harvest the pinot noir, that'll be something."

"Yes, he'll be mad as a wet cat if there's any delay in getting that land." Jeff laughed. "Though I don't think that he seriously expects you to default on the loan and lose the land."

"No, not even Bernie is that much of a fool," she agreed. "Have you ever had trouble with the IRS, Jeff?"

"No, we haven't. Of course," he said smiling, "they never have any trouble believing us when we say we're losing money. You know they don't audit people who can't pay the fines."

"Are you losing money?" Strangely, Hillary had never given much thought to the finances of a weekly newspaper.

"Yes, but we usually manage to break even by the end of the year." He winked at her, grinning. "As you can see, most of our profits go into my wardrobe."

Hillary smiled. His utilitarian wardrobe of long-sleeved shirts and jeans wasn't something she normally paid much attention to. He looked so perfect in any surroundings that she had never really noticed his casual attire.

"Do you ever think of getting out of the newspaper business?" she asked.

"What, and have to work for a living? No way."

"Seriously."

"Yes." He nodded, pursing his lips. "More often lately. But I'd never be able to sell the paper. I'd have to shut down if I quit."

"No one would buy it?"

"No. The small-town paper is a dying institution. The only way to make such a business truly profitable is with outside printing orders. Unfortunately, our presses are too old to handle that. If you can't print color photographs, you're out of luck these days."

"I never thought about it much," she admitted, patting his knee lightly. "A newspaper is just one of those things that you assume will always be there. It doesn't seem possible that yours would go out of business."

"I didn't say I was going out of business," he said. "Just that I was thinking about it. My father used to threaten to sell the paper at least twice a month when I was a kid. It's not an unusual sentiment for a newspaperman."

"Still, it does put things in perspective a bit." Hillary paused to suppress a yawn behind her fist. No matter how long she may have slept, it didn't feel as though it had been long enough. "I mean, no matter what's in our account books or how much trouble Bernie Foche causes me, I'm not worried about actually losing my business. It's not really possible, is it?"

"I don't know your balance, but I would think you're fairly safe."

"Right now, I could sell the whole thing," she said, looking seriously into his eyes. "But then it wouldn't be de Gaetano anymore. At least you've got cousins who might take over if you quit. There are no more of us."

"But my cousins aren't journalists," he reminded her. "They might be able to manage the finances, but they wouldn't be much good at writing the news. No, I'm afraid I'm the end of the line, too. Dad has told me time and again that if I want to close up the shop he won't hold it against me," Jeff explained. "But I don't plan to be the one who loses great-great-uncle Victor's newspaper. Or is it three 'greats'? I don't remember now."

"How are your parents?" Hillary said, changing the subject. "I haven't seen them yet." Again, she fought a yawn. Jeff's calm voice was so relaxing. She was so tired that she couldn't help enjoying the fuzzy warmth of the fatigue that was overcoming her.

"My folks are fine. In L.A. right now, but they'll be back next week."

"Boy, I'm tired," she said. "Maybe I'm coming down with something."

"Could be." Jeff leaned over and grasped her hand, squeezing. "You know, it's not required that you do everything yourself. You could get some rest and I'll see what the cops are up to."

"Would you? I'd like that," she said, failing to put much enthusiasm into her words. "I just don't feel up to talking to the police right now." She felt like sleeping, nothing more.

"I'd be glad to help. If I hear anything important, I'll call you."

"Thank you." Hillary stood, still holding Jeff's hand. Then she embraced him, holding him tightly to her. "I don't know what I'd have done without you helping me," she said.

"I just wish I could do more."

"Let's go." Releasing him, she started toward the door. "And I'll give you a key to the house, too. Just in case you can't wake me on some other morning. The way I feel, I could sleep through a war."

Jeff escorted her out feeling buoyed up by her words. It was good to be needed. It was the next best thing to being loved.

"I WANTED THE WORLD for you. And I would have given it to you."

The voice filled her head. It was hypnotically calm, and the words came in measured tones. The man seemed to have been speaking forever. She had no memory of anything before the presence of that melodic, caring voice.

"Love has never been an easy word for me," he said. "Never easy. Though I said it, I should have said it more often—every day, every hour. That might have been enough to show you my feelings."

There was a deep sadness in that voice, and Hillary wished she knew of some way to remove that tone of remorse and loss. But there was nothing she could do but listen while the oak tree whispered its encouragement overhead.

"Oh, Jeff," she sighed, in her dream.

Suddenly, as though her voice had broken an enchantment of some kind, the presence that had been there with her was gone. She could feel his absence. She was alone on the hill overlooking the vineyard. Completely alone.

The wind freshened slightly, chilling her exposed skin. In her dream, she sat and looked around her. The two main vineyard buildings stood below her, much as they did now, but without the third shed for harvesting equipment and without the asphalt roadway that now connected the buildings. A barn stood behind the main buildings. Hillary remembered it as a rickety old structure that had been torn down when she was a young girl. From her vantage point, she could see the old de Gaetano house beyond the slow rise of the vineyards, which were ripe with grapes. The house wasn't built in the Spanish mission style but was a large wood-frame structure, two stories with a porch on three sides. It stood where her ranch-style house stood now, but the old de Gaetano house had never stood in her lifetime. Her father had torn it down in the early fifties to make room for a smaller, more manageable house...her house.

She'd never actually seen that house!

Family photographs often included the porches, but there were no pictures of it in its entirety. How could she be seeing it now?

You're making it up, Hillary. You're just building on to what you've seen in old pictures. You are dreaming, after all.

But was she? Of course she was.

But it was the oddest, most detailed dream she'd ever had. As long as the man had been talking, she'd been willing to believe that it was a dream. It made sense then. But now, without the comforting sound of his voice, the whole thing seemed alien and threatening. Where was she? Why was she dreaming these things?

"Hello?" Standing, she called out to the man who had been speaking. "Hello?"

Everything was so clear. No matter where she turned or how quickly she moved, her vision never faltered. It all seemed absolutely real.

"Is anyone here?" Nobody answered.

The valley hadn't changed much. There were fewer roadways, and those that existed were only wagon tracks. And the town in the valley, normally just visible through foliage, was invisible to her from here. Other than that, things seemed very much the same. The vines, it seemed, were eternal. The vines were there through time, existing in her dreaming and waking worlds, providing an anchor for her mind. She clung to them now. It was all too real. She had never dreamed this realistically. Never.

"Hello! Where are you!"

There was no answer.

Hillary lifted the skirts of her long dress and began walking quickly down the hill toward the pressing building. It was important to get there, to find out why she was dreaming this strange dream. There had to be some reason.

"Where are you!" The frantic tone of her own voice startled her. She'd never been this frightened before. And she'd certainly never been this frightened by a dream. There had to be someone who could tell her what was going on. "Where is everybody?"

She seemed to be the only person in the whole world. There had to be someone else here. It was her dream; she could put someone in it if she wanted to.

"Come out and talk to me!" She stopped in the middle of a rutted track that ran through the vines. "It's *my* dream! Talk to me! Come out!"

Nobody answered.

"Wake up!" Suddenly, she didn't want to see anyone. She didn't want to know. All she wanted to do was to wake up and never sleep again. "Wake up! Wake up!" She screamed at the sky, trying to get the attention of her own conscious mind. She felt so totally alone. And she felt as if she might never wake up.

"Jeff! Jeff, help me!"

The sky was darkening overhead. Clouds moved in with an alarming swiftness and carried shadows as dark as night beneath them. Something terrible was coming. Something bad was going to happen to her here.

"Help me! Jeff! Jeff, please wake me up!"

But there was no reply as the clouds overtook her. There was no comforting touch of her friend's hand on her shoulder. But she felt something else approaching beneath the midnight veil of the clouds. Just as sure as she knew her own name, she knew that if she were to turn around now she would see what was approaching.

And she didn't dare turn to look for fear that it was her own death that she would see.

Behind her, came the sound of hoofbeats.

Chapter Nine

Jeff rang Hillary's doorbell at three o'clock. The police hadn't been very open about their investigation of either the murder or the tax matter. The latter, of course, was a federal concern, though it had been the local police who served the papers. All they'd said was that the federal authorities had brought their subpoena in that morning and they had acted on it immediately.

As to the murder, all they would tell either Jeff or Gil was that they had no suspects yet. They were waiting for the results of the autopsy and hoping that would provide a clue.

Jeff had gotten a better report from Lemuel Chambers, the detective in San Francisco. It was his information that had prompted Jeff to come back to Hillary's so soon. He knew she'd want to hear this as quickly as possible.

He rang the bell again and waited. There was no answer.

Could she really be that tired? She'd only been awake a few hours today. He knocked on the door, unsure of whether he wanted to use the key or not. Wandering in on her while she was sleeping seemed improper somehow, especially in light of his current feelings about her.

He smiled slightly as he took the key from his pocket, moving his fingers on it like a worry stone. Years of friendship had done nothing to help him with his newfound romantic feelings. He didn't know how to discuss them with her, or even if he should. Maybe it would be best for their friendship if he kept his mouth shut, but he knew it wouldn't be best for him to do so. He felt as though he were going to burst if he didn't tell her. In the end, he knew that he would have to do what was best for himself and hope that she might have some feelings for him in return.

Now, his problem was to get over his awkwardness, do what she'd suggested and open her door. She was obviously sound asleep. *Stop mooning here on the step and get with the program.*

He slipped the key into the lock, turned it, then pushed the door open. He was about to call for Hillary, but he stopped. What was that?

A moaning sound. It had been too low to be heard over the wind outside but was quite clear within the house. Hillary was moaning, as though she were in pain. Then Jeff heard a quick, sharp cry of alarm.

"Hillary!"

Jeff ran, leaving the door gaping open behind him. He slammed into her bedroom door before his hand found the knob. The force of the impact splintered the wood of the door frame; the door flew open and dumped him on his knees inside the room. He scrambled up, ready to do battle with whomever was assaulting Hillary.

But she was alone. Alone, lying beneath a sheet on her bed and moving restlessly. Tears poured down her cheeks.

"Hillary?" Jeff touched her shoulder.

"Wake up!" she shouted, rolling away from him. Her legs thrashed as though she were running, escaping something.

"Hillary!" Jeff grasped her shoulders firmly, rolling her back toward him and shaking her. "Wake up!" He echoed her words, shouting with an equal urgency. "Wake up!" Lifting her shoulders from the bed, he shook her so that her head lolled on her shoulders. "Wake up!"

Frantic now, he dropped the still-sleeping woman and ran to the bathroom for a glass of water. What on earth was wrong with her? She was totally out of it, locked away in the jail cell of her sleep. What if he couldn't wake her?

No, he wouldn't even contemplate a notion such as that. It was both too foolish and too horrible to think about. Of course he could wake her. She was only sleeping, wasn't she?

Wasn't she?

The small paper cup of water he brought back from the bathroom seemed terribly inadequate.

"Wake up!" He paused by her bed, shaking her with one hand.

Hillary only moaned.

Jeff threw the water at her face, hoping it would wake her and hoping she wouldn't think he was a total fool if he did.

HILLARY WAS RUNNING, her breath coming in a moan as she fought to get away from whatever was galloping behind her. She hadn't looked, hadn't dared to look. She only ran and hoped she would wake before it overtook her.

The dark clouds were gathering. The wind was rising.

"Wake up!" But she didn't know who she was yelling at. It was obvious that no one was listening.

Her pursuer was gaining. The hoofbeats grew so loud that she knew the horse would run her down in seconds, but the clouds broke and the rain hit her like a cold wave, washing away the landscape and muffling the sound of the horse.

After the rain, all that remained of her dream was a memory that was fading even as she focused on her bedroom and on Jeff's worried eyes.

"Jeff!" Hillary threw her arms around him so tightly that she pulled him off balance and full onto the bed. He was so warm and strong and real and alive. She wasn't dreaming and didn't ever want to dream again. "Hold me," she said with a sigh, enjoying the sound of her own voice almost as much as the feeling of the man she held in her anxious arms.

"Hold you?" Jeff laughed, his relief flooding out in sudden mirth. "You've got me pinned down, dear. I can't possibly hold you."

Hillary laughed, keeping him in her arms. He was lying across her legs, which were twisted in the sheets. When she did release him, it was only to grasp his face and kiss him quickly and passionately.

"Oh, what a dream," she said, blinking and wiping water from her eyes. "I didn't think I'd ever wake up."

"You didn't think you would? How could you know you were dreaming?" Jeff sat on the edge of the bed, found her hand and grasped it in both of his broad hands.

"I did, that's all. And I couldn't wake up for the life of me," she replied, unsure if she believed it herself. "I was on a hill overlooking the vineyards, but it was years ago. The old farmhouse was still there, not this one. Someone was talking to me and then he went away and I was alone. Then it began to get cloudy and I got scared and started running. And I couldn't wake up. Am I nuts or something?"

"No, you're just having nightmares. You're awake now, dear. I promise you that." Whatever he'd feared moments ago was forgotten now in the light of her smile. There was no anxiety in that smile. She was fine now. "To tell you the truth, I didn't think you were going to wake up, either," he said.

"Thank you for managing it, though." Hillary touched his cheek, marveling at the strength of his features and the compassion in his gentle eyes. Why hadn't she seen these things before? Why had he never looked this handsome to her when they were growing up together? "I see you called out the fire department to wake me," she said, glancing at the dampened sheets.

"Yes, but it seemed necessary when I couldn't shake you awake."

"Thank you. God, I was really out, wasn't I?"

"Maybe you should see a doctor, Hillary," Jeff said, more seriously. "I mean, this can't be good, can it?"

"I feel okay, Jeff."

"Yes, but no one sleeps that soundly."

"I'm fine," she insisted. She freed her legs from the sheets and swung them over the edge of the bed. "I've got to clean up now. Excuse me a moment."

"Sure," he said.

"So, can you leave so I can change clothes?" Hillary motioned toward the door, smiling slightly.

"Oh, okay." Jeff stood quickly, as though suddenly aware of their surroundings. "Say, I kind of wrecked your door on the way in," he explained as he walked out. "I can fix it easily later."

"I'll be out in a minute," she said, closing the door. "Make some coffee," she added through the slight crack as the door swung back open an inch.

"Right." Jeff retreated to the kitchen to prepare the coffee.

Hillary went to her bathroom and studied her face in the mirror. She didn't look too horribly bedraggled by sleep, not embarrassingly so, at any rate. Even as she checked her appearance, she laughed at the thought of primping for Jeff. A year ago she wouldn't have worried so greatly about how she looked to him. He'd seen her in a variety of unladylike conditions over the years. Surely his opinions of her were well formed by now. Still, she was glad she didn't look as flustered as she felt.

The dream was gone except for the feelings of fear and loneliness that lingered. Otherwise, all she could think of was how Jeff had broken down her door to wake her. He'd come to her rescue like a knight in a Sir Walter Scott novel.

If nothing else, this experience was teaching her the value of their friendship. Maybe that was a lesson she'd needed after so many years of taking their friendship for granted.

Jeff had apparently resolved to present a cheerful face to her when she came out to the kitchen a couple of minutes later. She knew him well enough to know that he hadn't dropped his opinion about seeing a doctor, but then he knew her well enough not to push it.

"So what brought you out here?" Hillary accepted a cup of black coffee and sat at the table.

"The police aren't saying anything," Jeff said. He stood by the sink with his cup in his hand. "They claim that they aren't ready to release anything about the murder to the press, and they don't know anything about the taxes. The feds brought them a warrant and they served it, that's all."

"No further explanation?"

"No."

"Do you think they've made any progress about Albert?"

"It doesn't seem as though they have." Jeff spoke reflectively, comparing this story against others in which he'd interviewed the police. "No, when they're making progress, they usually just say they haven't found anything. It's only when they're lost that they start making statements, as if they've got solid leads but just aren't willing to make them public."

"Who do we go to about the taxes?"

"Agent Carol Davis is handling the case out of the San Francisco IRS office. We'll have to go down there to talk to her."

"I can't go to the city now," Hillary protested. "Not with everything up in the air as it is."

"You might want to, anyway," Jeff suggested. He walked over to the table and sat, studying her face with his gently probing gaze. "I spoke to Lemuel Chambers," he told her. "He got some leads from those cabdrivers, and a couple of them seem to be panning out."

"Like the bank?" Hillary was skeptical about the probability of the answers being found in San Francisco.

"Yes, and that's one of the reasons for us to go to the city," he agreed. "The other lead is a guy named James Winger. I don't know anything about him, but Albert went to his address several times. It might be something."

"Or nothing," Hillary countered. "But I suppose we should get a look at the bank account. Does the IRS know about that?"

"I couldn't get any information about their investigation."

"I'd like to see about that before they do," she said. "Maybe it will explain what the problem is."

"Good idea. When do you want to go?"

"There's no time like the present. Care to take a little drive?"

"You don't seriously think I intended to stay here, did you?" Jeff laughed.

"Afraid you'll miss a good news story?" she teased.

"Darn right," Jeff said. "Besides, you never know when you might need me there to wake you up."

"Good point." Hillary adopted his light tone, though her heart raced. "I'd better keep you close at hand, Jeffery. Very close."

HE WATCHED THEM DRIVE to town with little interest. They stopped at the newspaper and then at a restaurant. But when they took the highway south out of town, he began to worry.

They were obviously going to San Francisco, and that wasn't where he wanted them to go. Whatever they might find there would only lead them farther from Bernard Foche and the justice that was due him.

Damn them! Why didn't they stay put? Why go wandering off now?

Obviously, it was Jeff who set them on this course. If he hadn't impulsively called in a private investigator they wouldn't have any reason to leave their initial course...the course he had worked so hard to put them on.

Jeff Simpson was getting in the way. He had been the one who'd awakened her, after all. Twice now he'd stood in the way of her dreams. He couldn't be allowed a third time.

The man was certain of that now. Despite their connection, he would have to do something about Jeff. If he could avoid killing him, that was fine. But, one way or another, Jeff had to be gotten out of the way. Only then would the woman be unprotected. Only then would she be his.

For now, he watched in useless frustration as Hillary's Mercedes convertible sped along the road to San Francisco and away from his influence. All he could do now was wait and perfect his plans. When they returned, he would be ready for them.

He would be ready for them all.

BERNARD FOCHE SAT BACK in his chair and rubbed his long fingers over his eyes. The last tour bus had gone an hour ago and the help had all gone home. It was degrading to be forced into letting tourists traipse over his land just to keep the place afloat.

Though it was still light out, he felt like calling it a day and going to bed. He would have gone, too, except for the nagging feeling that he'd left something undone. What it was, he had no idea, and that bothered him. He had been all too forgetful lately.

Normally a meticulous planner, Bernard had been having trouble concentrating for the last month. He'd been forgetting appointments and losing track of conversations. He'd delegated much more of his work than he liked, too. He felt overwhelmed for no apparent reason.

So what was it he had to do?

One thing he should have done was to bring that loan to Hillary's attention. Why hadn't he? He still didn't know. He didn't imagine that Albert had told her about it, and Bernard had fully intended to discuss it with her when he'd gone to see her. After all, no matter what had happened to Albert, business was business, wasn't it? Bernard had done good business with Albert, that was certain.

Still, once he'd seen Hillary, he just hadn't felt like doing business anymore. It had felt like someone clamped a hand over his mouth when he'd even thought of mentioning the loan. She'd think he was a weakling after that display. Well, she'd see how weak he was if she tried to default on Albert's loan.

It was legal. Completely legal. Bernard had seen to that fact, and there was no way she could avoid paying. Now he could only wait until de Gaetano Vineyard's financial condition became fully apparent to Hillary. When she knew just how badly strapped they were for cash, he would have the land. Then he'd have it all.

Bernard suddenly sat up, cocking his head toward the sound he thought he'd heard. No, it was nothing. But the lights flickered slightly, and he could feel a static charge in the air. Something was going to happen. What was it? Something . . .

The telephone rang, causing Bernard to jump in fright. He snatched the receiver and barked into it. "Hello!"

"They're going to San Francisco."

The voice on the line sounded terribly familiar, but Bernard couldn't remember if he'd really heard it before or not.

"They've taken her motorcar," the voice said. "They're taking wing, you might say." The caller hung up.

Bernard sat holding the receiver to his ear and staring blankly at a far wall. Then he replaced the receiver. He knew that voice, didn't he? Or had he only dreamed it? *Dreamed? Wasn't there something strange about his dreams?* He struggled to remember what the man had said. Why was San Francisco important? And what was that about "taking wing"?

Taking wing?

No, they couldn't have found out about that, could they? He'd taken care of that.

Bernard began flipping through his phone file, then stopped, pulling his wallet from his pocket instead and finding the number on a slip of paper inside. He picked up the phone again and dialed quickly. The phone rang several times before it was answered.

"Winger?" Bernard said. "Get him, then. It's Bernard."

While he waited, he drummed his fingers on the desktop and stared out the window at the fields. He'd grown up here, and now the damn vines were consuming his life, making their demands above and beyond anything he might have wanted for himself. Scrubland, all of it, he thought now. If it weren't for the wine country tours, he'd barely scrape by. The drought only emphasized what had been apparent all along: the Foche land wasn't good enough for a premium grape. It wasn't good enough land in which to bury his worst enemy.

If they had the land that was rightfully theirs, then they might yet attain something. If only they had the de Gaetano land! His family had been choking on "ifs" for as long as he could remember, but he was going to finally turn the "ifs" into "when." And "when" meant right now.

"Winger? Yeah, I think you're going to have company," Bernard said when the man finally came on the other end of the line. "The cousin just left for the city. Hillary de Gaetano. Don't worry, you'll recognize her. A tall blonde... yes, and she looks like she thinks she owns the world, too." Bernard scowled, thinking of Hillary and Jeff and their condescending attitude toward his whole family. "Yes, I'm sure you can take care of yourself. I'm just calling to say she's on her way. She'll probably have a guy with her, but he's nothing to worry about. She's the one with the money."

He hung up the phone, smiling now. Yes, she had the money for now. But between Winger and the IRS, she wouldn't have it for long. And then he'd hit her with the loan.

She'd had a homecoming to remember so far, but it wasn't over yet. No, it wasn't over by a long shot.

The lights flickered again, and the wind seemed to echo Bernard's laughter.

JEFF POUNDED on the frosted glass door of the detective's office, in a run-down building. The hall was dimly lit, the rows of doors waiting like gravemarkers along its walls.

"Real comforting location your investigator has here," Hillary commented, smiling.

"But Lemuel Chambers seems to get the job done," Jeff said.

"Except that he's late."

Hillary felt chilled by her surroundings, even though the night was warm. The seedy building and their uncertain mission in the city combined to depress her normally hopeful nature. All she could think to do was to check into a hotel and wait until morning. Maybe things would seem brighter after a good night's sleep.

But the thought of sleeping brought her around again. She definitely didn't feel like sleeping. In fact, her fatigue had dropped away since leaving home. Until this moment of uncertainty, she'd felt more awake than she had in days. Maybe it was just the sensation of movement that had brought her out of her shock, the sense that she was doing something. Or maybe it was her companion who brought out the best in her.

"Here he comes," Jeff said, breaking her train of thought.

Hillary turned to see a fat, middle-aged man waddling toward them down the hall. His tie was askew on his open collar.

"When you said eight, I didn't figure you meant a quarter of," he said as he came up to them puffing. He fished a key from the pocket of his light summer slacks. "I went to get a bite. Come on in."

"It is eight, Lemuel," Jeff said.

"Yeah, if you say so."

They followed Lemuel as he switched on the lights in a tiny anteroom and then unlocked the inner office door and ushered them inside. The fat man sat behind his desk with obvious relief and allowed himself to smile. "So, did you get to that bank account?"

"We'll have to go in the morning. We just got into town," Jeff said. He and Hillary sat on two wooden chairs in front of the desk. "This is Hillary de Gaetano."

"Yeah, pleased to meet you." But Lemuel didn't look pleased. He looked tired. "Say, I took this on your word, Simpson, but I really need a retainer to keep my self-respect. It's a money world out there, you know."

"I know," Jeff said, reaching for his wallet.

"No, this is mine." Hillary spoke firmly, tapping Jeff's shoulder. "Albert was my cousin."

"Hillary—"

"No," she said, taking her checkbook from her purse. "How much do I owe you, Mr. Chambers?"

"Five hundred," he said, licking his lips. "But I can't take a check."

"What?" Hillary stopped, her pen hovering over the checkbook. "My check is quite good."

"Sure, today it was," he said. "Don't get me wrong, because I trust you, but I try never to take checks from people with tax problems."

"How did you know?"

"Hey, you hired me to investigate, right? I tripped over that fact easily enough. A boy scout would have found that out without a compass, no sweat."

"But that doesn't affect my check," Hillary assured him.

"The IRS will freeze your assets as fast as you can blink, lady. I'll give you a word of advice," he said, fumbling a cigarette from the pocket of his jacket and lighting it. "If you've got money in checking, you should write it out to cash as soon as you can. Otherwise, you might not have anything to live on."

Hillary was about ready to explode with anger and embarrassment when Jeff spoke up, stopping her with a reassuring hand on her knee. "You'll take my check, won't you, Lemuel?" he asked. "My taxes are paid."

"Sure, I'll take your check. You two haven't talked to Davis, have you?" Lemuel asked. He watched Jeff write his check with great interest. "I tell you, she's hell in high heels, that's for sure. God's gift to the government, if you know what I mean."

"And you know that firsthand, do you?" Hillary asked, acidly. Lemuel's attitude about both the government and women was unnerving her. "Had your own tax problems?"

"Damn straight." The detective laughed, his jowls quivering happily. "I've had my fill of problems."

"But you were innocent, right?" Hillary said, scowling.

"No, guilty as sin." Chambers laughed again, reaching for the check that Jeff was holding out to him. "That's the last time I held anything back from Uncle Sam, too. And I don't ever want to deal with Carol Davis again."

Hillary couldn't help but smile now. The man was so uncouth that he was almost charming. He wasn't the type of man she was used to at all. Lemuel wore his thoughts on his sleeve rather than sheltering them behind polite words and gestures. Given time, she could even grow to like this fat, sloppy bear of a man. He was probably more trustworthy than most of the slick men she did business with.

"All right, Mr. Chambers," Hillary said. "We'll worry about the IRS tomorrow. We want to know about James Winger."

"Yeah, he's a sharpie." Lemuel folded Jeff's check and inserted it into the inner pocket of his jacket. He tapped the ash from his cigarette into an overflowing ashtray and sat back with a wary expression on his broad face. "Runs a sports book near Fisherman's Wharf. That and some crooked poker. I wouldn't gamble there, anyway."

"He's a gambler?"

"It's not gambling the way he does it." Lemuel laughed. "But then anybody who knows cards would stay away from his games. Only suckers play there."

"What about Albert?" she asked.

"Sorry, miss, but he was one of Winger's suckers. A big one, too, from what I can make out."

"How big?" Jeff cut in, concern creasing his forehead.

"You'll have to ask Winger that." The big man shrugged, grinding his cigarette out. "More than a few centuries, though. Thousands. I think we're talking big notes."

"I don't—" Hillary couldn't believe that about her cousin. Not her prudent cousin Albert. "Where did you hear this?"

"I've got some contacts. It wasn't just Winger, either. The way I heard it is that Winger was buying Albert's paper from other players who hadn't collected. He was paying ninety cents on the dollar, so he must have been pretty certain that it would pay off."

"Buying paper?" Hillary asked. He'd lost her now.

"Sure," the man explained. "IOUs. Your cousin lost bets with other bookies while he was betting on credit. Winger bought the IOUs from the bookies so he could collect on them himself. I figure that Albert must have been one of his regulars and Winger knew how to force him to pay all of it."

"Knew a way? Do you mean blackmail?" Hillary felt slightly ill. She was finding out too many things too fast.

"Probably. Gambling is illegal, you know. You can't take a guy to small claims court to collect, so you've got to have something on him to make sure he pays."

"Do you think that was why they let him gamble on credit?"

"Maybe. More likely, he had established credit because of his previous bets," the man explained. "Or he was letting previous winnings ride on more bets and got in over his head. I don't figure he could have gotten credit from so many places any other way. No, I'd say that Winger was the one he did most of his business with. He'd be the one guilty of blackmail."

"Maybe this IRS business was the leverage that Winger was using," Jeff suggested. "That bank account might be something."

"Might be," Lemuel agreed. "I didn't try getting into that since you had the next of kin on hand to do it. Did you people bring identification and all that for the bank?"

"Yes, we should have everything we need."

"Where is James Winger?" Hillary asked. "I want to talk to him."

"Not far from here," Lemuel said. "He owns some businesses that front for the gambling. Dry cleaners. A couple bars. His office is down at the Wharf Rat. It's a nice place. A tourist trap, but nice, anyway.''

"Let's go over there," Hillary said.

"Sure, no sweat. I don't suppose you people have anything to defend yourselves with."

"What, a gun?" Hillary asked. "Of course not."

"Too bad."

"Why should we need protection? It's a gambling matter," she said. "I'm sure we'll be fine."

"Yeah, but someone murdered your cousin," he pointed out. "Maybe it was Winger. If it was, he might decide that it's better business just to write off the debt and leave the both of you lying in a gutter somewhere."

"You can't really think that," Hillary insisted, even though she could see the logic in his warning.

"Sure I can," he said, shrugging. "Hell, you hired me to think of those things. There's nothing we can do about it now, anyway. I can't give you a gun. You might get picked up carrying it illegally and I'd lose my license. I tell you what, when you're on Winger's turf just agree to whatever he says. Gamblers don't want trouble. Don't make waves, and he probably won't make any, either."

"That sounds like good advice," Jeff said.

Lemuel pushed himself up from his chair. He reached inside his jacket and adjusted his own weapon in its holster under his left arm. "I have a gun, though Lord knows I'm no fast draw. Come on."

"Are you coming, too?" Hillary had gotten the distinct impression that they were to make this trip on their own.

"You paid for today," he said simply. "Today ain't over yet. I'm only wishing it was."

Right then Hillary was wishing it was over, too.

Chapter Ten

The Wharf Rat wasn't the seedy dive that its name implied. It was a large, polished lounge featuring a stage show, and it sat on the corner of a block near the wharf. A large neon sign ran the length of the establishment, calling out to patrons in pink-and-blue letters. It appeared to be a popular place, too, if the number of people going in and out was any indication.

The three of them got out of Hillary's Mercedes at the entrance to the parking lot. Hillary handed her keys to the attendant, and Lemuel Chambers led them into the lounge.

A young man in a tuxedo was singing "It Had to Be You" beside a piano at center stage with drum and bass accompaniment. The tables were full of well-dressed patrons who listened and talked quietly in the large main room. The hostess led them to seats near the back wall, at one of only a few remaining tables, and promised to send a waitress for their order.

"This is hardly a 'wharf rat' type of place," Jeff commented, looking around the room casually. "A name like that makes you expect something horrible."

"It would depend on your purpose for coming here," Lemuel said. "If you're here for the floor show and a couple drinks, it's a fine place. If you're here to gamble, it's horrible."

Hillary laughed. Her darker fears had been mollified, and she was no longer worried about having any trouble with James Winger. As was apparent from his place, he was a businessman, and a businessman, like a gambler, wouldn't want trouble.

The waitress came for their order. The heavy detective ordered a Scotch on the rocks while Jeff ordered Irish coffee. Hillary thought for a moment, then said, "I'd like some wine. Do you have de Gaetano Chablis?"

The waitress smiled, nodding. "I think we may have," she said. "You must be here to talk to Mr. Winger."

"How did you know that?" Hillary asked.

"Except for Mr. Winger's friend, Al, people don't order wine by name here very often," she explained. "Besides, de Gaetano is a pretty fancy wine for people traveling with a private detective."

Lemuel laughed, answering Hillary's questioning look by saying, without apology, "I used to gamble in my youth. Before my tax problems."

"Yes, we would like to see Mr. Winger," Jeff said. "When he's free."

"I'll tell him," she replied, turning toward Hillary. "We don't sell de Gaetano by the glass. You'll have to buy a bottle."

"Bring the bottle then," Lemuel cut in. "Cancel my Scotch. I'll have wine."

"Might as well cancel my order, too," Jeff put in.

"Yes," Hillary said. "A bottle would be fine."

After the waitress left, Jeff turned to Hillary and laughed. "We're in for a heck of a markup, Hill. You should have just brought a bottle from home."

"Relax Jeff," she said. "Let's have a night on the town while we're at it."

"I'm with you," he said, his eyes lighting briefly with a fire other than that of the quest that had brought them here. There was a warmth in that light that seemed to heat her cheeks as he looked at her.

The pianist was playing a medley of Gershwin numbers when their wine arrived. "It's on the house," the waitress said as she placed the glasses in front of them. "Mr. Winger will be by soon."

"We must really rate," Hillary said, letting Jeff pour the wine. "Or else Mr. Winger expects to earn some money tonight."

"Whatever happens," Lemuel cautioned, "don't make waves."

The three of them lifted their glasses in a toast and sipped, each watching the room around them for some sign of the owner's approach.

"This is pretty good," the portly detective commented, smiling at his glass. "I must be getting old. Never liked wine much when I was a youngster. What am I supposed to do, swirl it around in my mouth or something?"

"No," Hillary said, laughing. "Just drink it. Too much study ruins the mystery of wine and makes it hard to simply enjoy it. Albert was our wine expert. He could tell you the exact composition of almost any glass of wine he tasted."

"Composition? Wine's just grapes, isn't it?" Lemuel asked.

"Yes, but different grapes taste differently, so you blend grapes to achieve the final taste you want," she explained.

"Well, there's something I didn't know before," Lemuel said. "Here's to good wine." He lifted his glass in another toast.

"Drink up," Jeff said. "It's free."

"Yes, and I'll send more, if you wish." A tall, slender man in a business suit approached the table. "I am James Winger," he said. "You must be Hillary."

He was a dapper-looking man who wore his blond hair combed back against his narrow skull. Observant blue eyes peered out past a squat nose that didn't seem to fit his otherwise-lean face. When he smiled, he showed his teeth.

"Yes, I'm Hillary de Gaetano," she said, half rising and extending her hand. "And this is Jeff Simpson and Lemuel Chambers."

"I know Mr. Chambers," he said. He turned to shake Jeff's hand. "And you are the newsman Albert mentioned."

"Yes," Jeff acknowledged, returning the man's unwavering gaze and the pressure of his handshake in kind.

"Please, take a seat, Mr. Winger." Hillary motioned to an empty chair. "Would you care to join us in some wine?"

"Thank you, but I don't drink during business hours." He seated himself and casually crossed one leg over his knee.

"That's a good policy," Hillary said.

"You seem to know a lot about us," Jeff said, his tone remaining light and conversational.

"Albert was here fairly regularly. We spoke often."

"That's why we're here," Hillary said. "You have probably heard that Albert is dead."

"Yes, in the papers. I'm terribly sorry."

"It was a great shock," Hillary said. "We're in the process of putting his affairs in order at the moment. Your name came up along the way."

"Yes, well, Albert and I did have dealings," he said, nodding. "But nothing very large, I assure you."

"Good. That's what we were hoping to hear," she said. The man certainly seemed to be telling the truth. At least, nothing in his demeanor gave any indication of subterfuge. "Did Albert do a great deal of gambling with you?"

"With me? Or at my tables?" He spoke without pause, still smiling.

"Either one."

"Not what I would call a lot. He wasn't a very good card player, and he knew it. Unfortunately, win or lose, he enjoyed the game, so he did play from time to time. Horse races and sporting events tended to be kinder to him."

"Really? Do you have a sports book here?" Jeff spoke quickly, more on reporter's instinct than thought.

"For the record, Mr. Simpson, no, I do not." Winger smiled broadly, shrugging. "Do I, Chambers?" he asked the detective, who had remained silent.

"Nobody has proved you run a book, if that's what you mean," Lemuel said. "But we don't really care, anyway. We just want to know how much the guy owed you."

"Ah, tactless as usual," Winger said. "Miss de Gaetano, let me put your mind at ease. Your cousin didn't owe me anything. His debts here were all paid in full. As to anyone else to whom he may have owed money, I can't say."

"But weren't you buying his papers?" Hillary asked.

"Some," he admitted easily. "Business is business, after all. But, as I said, Albert didn't owe *me* a cent."

"That's a relief, anyway," Lemuel said, finishing his second glass of wine. "Do you know of anywhere else he may have gambled?"

"No. I went with him to the track several times, but I do not book bets on races."

"It looks as though you do quite well with this," Hillary pointed out. "I wouldn't think you'd need gambling to make money."

"You're absolutely right," Winger said. "Gambling built this for me. Now that it's all here, I find the gaming to be a liability. Bribes are costly."

"You sure are open about it," Jeff said. "What's to stop me from reporting it in my paper?"

"Nothing," he said. "But reporting it and proving it are two different things. Besides, you're not exactly running a national paper."

"Right," Jeff said, returning the man's smile. "And I'll bet you could come up with a pile of associates who were here at the table with us to prove that you never admitted any of that to us."

"Of course."

"How much did Albert owe you?" Hillary said. "In round numbers."

"Owe me? He owed me nothing."

"But how much did he pay you, Mr. Winger? How long did he gamble here?"

"Gamble? My goodness, Miss de Gaetano," the man said, coolly. "There's no gambling here. Gambling is illegal."

"Yes, but how..." Hillary let her question trail off. He wasn't about to answer that question. "Oh, never mind."

"Your cousin was a great guy," Winger said. "Life of the party around here. I'd like to remember him in a good light. Gambling to excess is a vice. I think a man's vices should be buried with him."

"Did he gamble to excess?" Jeff asked.

"Yes, I would say that he did," the man replied without hesitation. "But you don't really want to dwell on that now, do you?"

"No, we don't," Hillary said. "Thank you for your time."

"I hope no one dwells on my vices," Lemuel suddenly said, laughing. "But, with my luck, they'll chisel them into my tombstone."

"I must get back to work now," Winger said, standing. "Anything you want is on the house tonight. It's the least I can do."

"Yes, thank you," Jeff said, shaking his hand.

"Good night," Hillary said to the departing bar owner.

"Good night. It's been a pleasure meeting all of you," he said. Then he turned and walked away, leaving them sitting quietly.

"You messed up with that reporting stuff," Lemuel said after a moment. "You put him on guard."

"No," Hillary said. "I don't think he would have told us how much money Albert lost here, anyway."

"No, even if he did, he could easily deny it later. I wonder why he didn't tell you," Jeff said.

"Probably because he doesn't want you to know," Lemuel said.

"Yes, there's a lot of secrecy going around. Just like Bernie Foche not telling me about that loan, though I'll bet he's been looking forward to springing the news since I got back." Hillary contemplated her new information somberly. Albert's gambling was news enough, but Bernie's reticence to collect money was earthshaking.

"Foche?" Lemuel scratched his head. "Skinny guy? Going bald? Hook nose? Down from the Napa Valley?"

"Yes, that's him. Do you know him?" Jeff leaned forward, curiosity stiffening the whole of his muscular form.

"He's been here. I know that much about him," Lemuel said. "That's about it. I've seen him around many times."

"Here? In this club?" Hillary asked. "Did he know Winger?"

"I couldn't say," the detective said. "Lots of people come in here who don't know the owner."

"Yes," she said, feeling let down slightly. "It's probably nothing."

Lemuel checked his watch and then pushed his chair back with a sigh. "I'd better take off now. Unless you people have other places to go this evening."

"No, nowhere until tomorrow," Hillary said. "Thank you."

"I'll call if we need anything else, Lemuel," Jeff said. "Thanks for your good work."

"Yeah, well I've been paid for it. Good night all."

The man waddled off with a small salute, disappearing into the crowd.

"So, what now?" Jeff asked. "It's only ten o'clock."

"I think that we might as well take our host up on his offer," Hillary said. "I seem to remember that you know how to dance, Jeff."

"Last time I tried I did, anyway," he said. "Shall we give it a go?" He stood, extending a hand toward her.

"I'd love to," she said, laughing. It felt good to push off her cares, if only for an evening. And since they couldn't do anything further until the morning, they might as well enjoy themselves now.

As she rose to be escorted to the dance floor, she realized that Albert's death had taught her one valuable lesson. She shouldn't waste the time she had, for there was no telling when that time might run out.

DESPITE HIS BULK, Lemuel Chambers was light on his feet and usually managed to move unobtrusively when he wished to. So he was able to slip into Winger's outer office without being heard. He was able to hear Winger making a phone call, and what was said didn't please the big detective very much. He'd have to investigate first, but things seemed to be making more sense now.

He slipped out of the office as carefully as he'd come in, but, unfortunately, not unseen. A slick-looking man in a suit watched him leave and then hurried into the office to tell Winger. Moments later, the man emerged from the office and called another man to join him, and they left the club through a side door to the alley.

Lemuel wasn't able to attract the first cab that passed outside the club, so he began walking. He hadn't far to go, but he was unaccustomed to walking any great distance, so he would have preferred a cab. With that in mind, he stopped at the mouth of the alley nearest the club and scouted the street for transportation. A yellow cab turned the corner at the far end of the block and approached him.

He was just about to step from the curb to hail it when a muffled pop sounded. He staggered, reaching for the building wall for support. His hand slipped on the bricks, his knees buckled, and he fell to his face on the sidewalk.

Fortunately, two patrons were leaving the club when he fell. A man shouted in alarm and ran toward the fallen detective while his companion rushed inside to summon help. The dark figure in the alleyway stepped back quickly and disappeared into the shadows. If the first shot hadn't been enough, he wouldn't have another chance now.

"Foche," Lemuel Chambers whispered urgently to the man who was trying to hold him still on the sidewalk. "Got to warn them," he added. "Warn about Foche."

That was all he said before passing out. It would be several days before the detective would be conscious enough to speak that warning again. By that time, it would be too late.

THE ENTERTAINERS ON STAGE continued with a pleasant mix of danceable vocal and instrumental music, and Hillary and Jeff took several turns on the dance floor. Dancing close and slow, they began somewhat shyly before letting the rhythm of the music take them along its own avenues of feeling.

Hillary found herself feeling strangely nervous to be this close to Jeff. Their friendship had never included social engagements of this sort, not with each other, at any rate. They'd double-dated in high school, of course, but their interaction since then had usually concerned work and occasional dinners when Hillary was in the valley. But now, with her newfound sense of Jeff's physical presence, Hillary was admiring things about him that she'd never seriously contemplated before.

Now, while they danced to the music of Cole Porter and Gershwin, she became aware of every small contact between their bodies. Every shifting movement of the dance created a warmth within her, and the pressure of his hands holding her was both comforting and exciting. It had been too long since she'd allowed herself to have fun like this, too long since she'd been out for reasons other than business. She found herself totally enthralled with the enjoyment of being with a man again.

Jeff Simpson was as much man as she could handle. She knew that he was all the man she would ever want or need, too. It was strange how she'd not noticed that before. Though each of his many attributes had always been apparent to her, she'd never put them together and studied him as she might any other man. Jeff was always her friend. He was a man of strength, or grace, or intellect or humor, but never quite all at one time. It was as if she'd been enjoying only certain aspects of him over the years, and then just when it suited her purposes.

Now, as they danced, she found herself regretting the years she'd never connected her favorite things about him into a unified whole. She regretted not knowing he could make her feel this way.

Did he feel the same way? She couldn't be sure. The way he was looking at her—had been looking at her since her return, for that matter—seemed to indicate that he did. As outgoing as he was, she felt that he might suffer from the same doubts she did. He, too, might be reluctant to spoil a friendship with demands for a deeper relationship.

They continued drinking the bottle of wine they'd begun with the detective, sitting between dances while trying to occupy themselves with impersonal talk. It wasn't easy, and Hillary found herself losing track of their conversation. Her eyes wandered over his broad chest or concentrated on the muscular width of his hands. There were so many things to imagine about him. So many things to imagine about the two of them together.

"I doubt Bernie's coming here means anything," Jeff was saying. "It doesn't look as though there's any connection between Winger and Albert's death at all."

"What? Oh, no, it doesn't." Hillary smiled wanly, trying to concentrate. "And Bernie may be a snake, but he's not a murderer."

"He doesn't have the gumption to do much more than whine," Jeff added. Even as he spoke, his eyes were disconnected from his words. They had moved over her face, her body, with increasing abandon as the evening moved on. "What about that bank account? Do you think we'll find the answers there?"

"How could we? We don't know the questions yet. With everything in such a mess, and with the IRS snatching our files, I haven't been able to go over the books to see if there's really anything irregular."

"You don't think Albert was doing something to the books?" Jeff's gaze lost its dreaming expression; he focused on her face.

"I wouldn't have thought he did much gambling a couple days ago, but he did," she said sadly. "We're going to have to face up to a lot of disagreeable facts before this is finished.''

"Yes. It's a hell of a thing when a person dies before they put their house in order," Jeff said. "Outsiders can read most anything into the things left behind.''

"And, in this case, he left tax problems and a loan with Bernie. Beyond that, we have no clue." She didn't want to talk about this anymore. Albert was dead, but she was alive. She couldn't bring him back to life and couldn't solve any of her difficulties tonight. Tonight was for dancing.

Hillary stood resolutely. She wasn't going to waste this opportunity. Never again in her life would she allow a personal opportunity to pass her by.

"Dance with me again, Jeff," she said. "We'll take care of business tomorrow."

This time they moved in concert with each other as though they'd been dancing as a team for years. His every movement was mirrored by her body moving close to his. She could feel the muscles in his legs tense and relax with the songs; his chest moved with the breath that tickled her neck while they danced. And, perhaps in answer to her unasked questions, she could feel his physical response to her. Moving as close as they did, she couldn't help but notice that telltale sign that his thoughts were running in tandem with hers.

At the end of the song, they stopped dancing but didn't part. Instead, they stood looking into each other's eyes, their breath mingling in the brief space between them. Hillary smiled, cocking her head slightly to admire the play of the sedate lighting on his features. Wordlessly, she reached one hand up to touch his cheek.

Jeff responded by tightening his grip on her back and pulling her firmly against him. Then he dipped his head to bring his lips slowly down to meet hers. It was a brief but passionate kiss, his tongue moving lightly and retreating. Hillary pushed herself up on her toes to reassert contact, and the second kiss claimed them as though the kiss were everything.

Hillary gave herself entirely to the kiss and let its hungry heat move through her body. The feeling of her breasts rubbing against the fabric between them and the excitement of their hips pressing firmly together was overwhelming. It wasn't possible that he didn't share her feelings. And, even if he didn't feel exactly the same, Hillary was too far into the kiss to turn back now.

It was Jeff who broke the kiss. Smoldering desire flickered in his blue eyes. The music had begun again, but they didn't move. "I think that's enough dancing for tonight," he said.

"The night's young," she said. Was he going to back away from her? Was she wrong about him? "What should we do now?"

"I want to go to our hotel." His voice was low and sensuous and very serious. He spoke as a man who knew exactly what he wanted and wasn't afraid to admit it. And, in the measured tone of his words, Hillary found the reassurance she had sought.

"Yes." Her heart was beating so hard that her breath was constrained. "It's time to go back to the hotel," she agreed.

They turned without further talk, stopping at the table only long enough to leave a tip for their waitress. No matter what their mission had been when they'd first come to the Wharf Rat, the place had come to hold a far different significance in their lives.

On the drive back to the hotel, Hillary could barely concentrate on the traffic, not with him so near her; she didn't dare touch him for fear of losing control. Was this love? Really love, after all this time?

Going into the hotel and upward in the elevator, Hillary had a guilty feeling, as if the desk clerk was watching them. Could he tell that the couple who had checked in earlier and who had insisted on a suite with two bedrooms had changed their intentions in the intervening hours? It seemed as though he could.

It was so beautiful to feel as she felt now that any such foolishness was possible.

"Jeff, I—" Hillary began when they reached the suite.

He cut her off with a kiss and pushed the door closed behind them. His tongue probed her mouth as though he had to savor every sensation.

"Okay," he said, breaking the kiss. "I had to do that before you might tell me it's all a mistake."

"It's not a mistake," she said simply.

"Are you sure? It's not the wine talking?"

"No, it wasn't the wine that gave me the idea. Kiss me again, Jeff."

He didn't need a second command but claimed her lips. He held her tightly to him in a possessive embrace. Then he bent and picked her up. "Do you have a preference of rooms?" he whispered.

"Any room with a bed in it will do just fine." She kissed him as he walked; she found it impossible to keep her lips away from him now that they'd found privacy.

He kicked the bedroom door shut behind them, carrying her to their destination. Then he placed her carefully on the bed and stood looking at her.

"You're beautiful, Hillary," he said. "I've been dying to say that for some time now."

"Why did you wait?" Hillary began unbuttoning her blouse.

"No," he said, leaning one knee on the bed and stopping her hand. "Let me do that."

"Oh, yes," she said with a sigh. Dropping her hands, she let him finish. He unclasped her bra.

"I never thought this was possible," he said.

The gentle touch of his fingers on her breast, followed by his lips and tongue, tormented Hillary. She desperately wanted to pull him closer, but she lay still, enjoying his touch. This was too good to rush, so perfect that it had to last.

When he'd finished undressing her, her body seemed to shine in the moonlit room. Hillary felt his desire wash over her like a wave of longing. And she knew that his feeling not only mirrored hers but predated hers. He'd been aware of his need for her long before she'd become aware of him. She had never felt this wanted or this loved in her life, and she had never wanted or loved any man this much.

The sight of his body, glimpsed between kisses as he struggled out of his own clothes, had inflamed her further. His lips and hands gave tempting previews of what was to come, bringing out responses from her body that she'd never known were possible. Finally naked with him, she let him traverse her body with his hands and his mouth.

Flesh on flesh, they moved with a familiarity attained only through years of acquaintance. The friendship they'd both worried would stand in the way was in their favor now, allowing them a freedom from the awkwardness that might have accompanied the culmination of their love.

Hillary kissed down his chest hungrily, grasping him as she neared the center of his desire while he inflamed her own desires. Each movement was artfully countered as they rolled on the bed, exalting in the pleasure they were able to give each other. Their bodies were a feast, the taste of which neither had known before.

Now Jeff moved above her, his hand creating pure pleasure with the simplest movements. His lips traversed her throat, found her mouth and claimed it. Their tongues danced in rhythm to the pulse of their unmet desires.

"Oh, Jeff," she gasped, throwing her head back with a throaty chuckle. "I want you now, darling. I—I can't wait."

Jeff rolled away from her. "Just a second," he said, leaving the bed.

"What?" she called out, watching his moonlit form.

"Protection," he said simply when he returned. "Thank God hotels plan ahead even if I don't."

A moment later, he was holding her tightly to him again, moving on top of her. And his movement began as a silken feeling within her, each thrust a pulse of joy that deepened as it grew more urgent and more powerful. Their release had no beginning and no ending, it simply was—existing as a perfect moment in time—and it left them both immobile and locked to each other as though afraid to break the spell by even daring to breathe.

Finally he turned, lying at her side with a satisfied sigh. "Beautiful," he said. "That was, and you are, beautiful."

"I never expected this when I came home," Hillary said, kissing his cheek. She smiled. "Oh, Jeff, we should have done this years ago."

"I thought about it a time or two," he admitted, forcing himself to sit on the edge of the bed. "I never thought it would actually happen."

"When did you first think about us? How long ago?" She accepted his embrace, savoring the feeling of his arms around her.

"Years ago," he replied, pausing to kiss her cheek.

"Why didn't you tell me then?"

"You had a fairly steady guy then, Hill," he said. "I wasn't about to try breaking you up."

"Why not?"

"Because you were happy." He kissed her again, stroking his hand gently over her hip. "I didn't want to lose a friend."

"Why admit it now?" She returned his kiss, feeling the desire that had seemed sated moments before grow within her again.

"I guess I finally admitted to myself that I wasn't going to get over it. It was now or never." He rubbed his hand over her back and then massaged her neck. "What about you? Why tonight?"

"Ever since I came home I've been seeing you differently, Jeff," she said. "Before this week, I had never really considered just how much I rely on you. I need you. You seem like part of me, somehow. Do you know what I mean?"

"Yes, I do." He kissed her throat. "Even before I was aware of it, there was nobody I wanted but you."

"Yes, exactly. That's why no relationship ever lasted for me." She laughed. "Because those other guys weren't you. I needed someone I could depend on, someone I could trust, as well as someone I could laugh with. They might have been one of those things, but not all of them. You have always been the only one who was all of those things."

"I love you, Hillary. I always have."

And, just as though they'd always been together, they resumed their lovemaking with joyous abandon. It was as if they'd always known the truth about the nature of their friendship.

The night was all too short to contain their love, but when they finally drifted off to sleep, they slept secure in the knowledge that they could have countless nights like this to reassert the love that bound them. They would have every night in existence from now on.

Chapter Eleven

Hillary awakened to darkness and a feeling of disorientation. Jeff's hand resting on her hip as he slept, brought her memories back and gave her a sense of security she'd lacked upon waking. Feeling him lying close behind her, his arm protectively over her, made her feel cozy again. She knew where she was now.

She stared into the darkness of the hotel bedroom and allowed her mind to wander over the strange chain of circumstances that had led to this moment. Her strange dreams, Albert's death, the discovery of his trips to the city and his connection to the club near the wharf seemed like an inevitable progression now. It was as if everything was foreordained, including this new revelation of love. And, even as Albert's death made her aware of the tenuous nature of life, her changed relationship with Jeff made her feel that some things could last forever. It was strange how things worked out.

But would they work out? Would they ever capture Albert's killer? What about the IRS? There were so many things to worry about that she almost felt ashamed for enjoying herself so thoroughly tonight. Almost.

Life and death coexisted by necessity. She was alive and deserved happiness if she could find it. She deserved it every bit as much as Albert had deserved to remain alive, and she couldn't bring him back by denying herself Jeff's love.

Life was so horribly precious just then. Life was so beautiful. Hillary couldn't help the tear that trickled from her eye when she thought of how beautiful her life had suddenly become. If only Albert were still alive. Then her life would be perfect.

As HILLARY DRIFTED off to sleep again, Gil Dickinson was using a credit card to work past the lock on Albert's back door. The police had been very unsympathetic to his requests to see the files in the house. He wasn't family, after all; he was just a nosy reporter.

But Gil had a hunch about those files, and he had become so consumed by his thoughts on the matter that he'd given in and come to see them for himself. If he was right, Hillary wouldn't mind that he'd broken in. And the police would be pleased to have their murder case wrapped up once they figured out a way to claim credit for solving it.

After getting the door open, Gil slipped into the kitchen and then up to the office on the second floor. There had to be some medical records in there... something to tell him if he was on the right track.

He paused on the second-floor landing, sensing something unusual about the house. It felt as if he wasn't alone. But then the feeling passed through him like a breeze. He was just nervous. That was all.

It was probably foolish taking this route, but Hillary and Jeff would be out of town most of tomorrow, and he couldn't wait that long for permission to search the files. He didn't have any concrete reason to check, just a hunch, but that was enough. After nearly forty years, Gil Dickinson's hunches were generally strong enough to hold up in court.

The only problem with this hunch was that he didn't know what name to look under. He decided to look for receipts first. That might give him a clue.

He had turned on a green-shaded desk lamp and was sorting through the papers in the file cabinets when he heard a thump in the hall. Shoving the drawer shut quickly, he turned, switched out the light and waited, holding his breath.

Had someone seen the light from the street and called the police? Gil wasn't eager to spend the night in a jail cell for his efforts. When a moment passed without incident, he turned the light on again, frowning. If it had been the police they wouldn't have waited for an invitation. They would have just come in and been done with it. It was just his imagination.

Before he could return to his surreptitious task he heard more noise outside the office door. It sounded like footsteps.

This time, Gil left the light on and walked to the office door. They probably knew who he was and were having some fun with him. The local police weren't known for their humor, but it was probably too good a chance to turn down.

"Hello," he said, opening the door. "If there is anyone out here, why don't you quit playing games and come on in?"

The hall seemed empty at first. The desk lamp cast a feeble rectangle of light across the hall to the other wall, giving the hallway a dim glow. Nobody was there. But then there was somebody, a man.

Gil had stepped into the hallway and was standing at the head of the stairs when he saw the man in the black coat at the far end of the hall. The man wore a black hat. A bolo tie was secured around the collar of his white shirt. He took a step toward the newsman, appeared to be reaching out to him, and then he disappeared.

The man just vanished, leaving Gil staring into the empty darkness, wondering if the man had really been there at all. He'd better finish up and get out of here, he thought. The place was giving him the creeps.

When he turned back to the office, the man was there again, now blocking the door with his dark form. Dark, but not entirely dark, for the dim light seemed to be shining through him like a projection on glass. He glowed slightly from the light, his face lit like a white neon mask.

And then the vision moved, reaching for Gil with a hand that couldn't be real, not with the light shining through it. But it grabbed him with real-enough strength, shoving him against the wall.

Gil felt a sudden, unreasoning terror. He didn't want the man to touch him again. He ran toward the stairs and slipped on the top step, only keeping himself from falling headlong by grabbing the railing at the last moment. One glance upward told him that the vision was still there.

Gil ran down the stairs, his heart hammering within his chest. He pulled frantically at the front door before remembering that he'd come through the back and that this door was locked. Behind him, the man had reached the bottom of the stairs and was walking toward him. Gil unlocked the door with stiff fingers, threw it open and ran out. He was on the street before he stopped running. He turned to look back with his heart still hammering loudly in his ears.

The man stopped in the doorway, paused for a moment to return Gil's stare, and then he disappeared again. After the vision was gone, the front door slammed shut. A moment later, the light in the upstairs office was extinguished.

The street seemed quite normal now. The streetlights glowed at the intersections, and the houses lay in dark slumber along either side. Gil swallowed hard, trying to stop his hurried breath, trying to convince himself that it was all his imagination.

That was something he couldn't do. He didn't know what it was, but he did know that it wasn't his imagination. And he also knew that he wasn't about to go back into that house again. Not now, not even in daylight. Whatever was in there wasn't playing games.

Something in Albert's house had been deadly serious about keeping him out.

CAROL DAVIS SUCCEEDED in ruining Hillary's wonderful mood before she and Jeff were even let into the IRS office. She did that by making them wait for nearly an hour in the bland, impersonal reception area even though they'd called ahead for an appointment. By the time they were led inside, Hillary was predisposed to disagree with her on every point of their discussion. As it turned out, she would have disagreed no matter what her mood had been.

Agent Davis was a small woman in a well-tailored suit who spoke and moved with very precise movements. She was of average good looks, but the serious pinch of her lips removed any hint of friendliness from her features. She wasn't the type of person Hillary would willingly deal with. Now, however, she had no choice.

"I'm not really at liberty to say much about our investigation at the moment," Agent Davis said. She shook her dark hair back with an authoritarian air, smiling without friendliness at the two people seated across the desk from her. "It isn't completed, as you know. We don't like to release findings until we've checked them."

"But it concerns me," Hillary pointed out. "I should think that I'm allowed to hear what I'm supposed to have done wrong."

"Not you, Ms. de Gaetano. Your late cousin is the one under investigation. He and the winery."

"Which means me, Ms. Davis. As you just said, my cousin is dead. His share of the business is mine automatically."

"Is that a provision of his will?"

"No, it's not an inheritance. We always owned the business equally."

"But you split the operations down the middle. We're not investigating your financial business, only the winery and Albert's management of it."

"But it's my winery," Hillary insisted. The woman's officiousness was too much to bear. "I deserve to be told the charges."

"When there are charges, you'll surely be told. Though I believe that the warrant cited tax evasion."

"That's broad," Jeff cut in. "Are you charging the winery with outright fraud? Miscalculations? Misinterpretation of the tax laws? Or are you just fishing?"

"I can tell you that we acted on a tip when we seized the records," the woman said. "At this point, we don't have any specific charges."

"A tip? Who tipped you? When?" Hillary couldn't believe the charges to begin with, let alone that someone might have called the IRS.

"I can't go into that. You do understand."

"No, I don't understand. You can't just make accusations without giving some cause." Hillary spoke with tight calmness, but it was hard to maintain her reasonable facade.

"You are not being charged with anything," the woman said now in a smooth tone. "It is your cousin we're investigating."

"Yes, but it's my business," Hillary repeated.

"Only Albert de Gaetano's personal activities are being questioned."

"But you took the company records," Jeff said. "As far as I know, you didn't take his personal records."

"If his personal records hadn't been burned, we would have taken them," the agent pointed out. "That in itself should say something about the validity of the investigation."

"What? Do you think Albert burned his own files?" Hillary was incensed, her anger straining to make itself heard.

"That wouldn't be inconsistent. He was heavily in debt to gamblers. A great deal of the company records were burned, as well."

"How could he have burned them if he was dead?" Hillary stood, glaring down at the woman sitting behind the large desk. "That makes no sense!"

"As I understand it, the estimates as to time of death allow plenty of leeway for him to have started the fire and returned to his office. He would hardly have stayed around to watch them burn."

Hillary threw up her hands in exasperation. There was no getting around this woman, not at all. "Let's get this straight," she said. "You won't tell us the charges because, even though they involve my company, they don't concern me?"

"As I've said, nobody is charging you with anything."

"But you're investigating me!"

"We're investigating your cousin."

"Who is dead! You're investigating his operation of part of our family business. Am I not part of the family?"

"Certainly you are."

"Then tell me what the charges are."

"There are no charges," the woman said again. "Until we bring charges, we don't need to say anything about them."

Hillary could see right then that the whole visit had been pointless. She might as well have been talking to a rock.

"All right." Jeff stood, smiling tiredly. "We might as well go. He extended his hand to Agent Davis. "Thank you. Come on, Hillary."

"Should you decide what you'd like to charge us with, you can call our lawyer." Hillary turned and walked to the door. Jeff held it open, and they left the room without waiting for a reply.

"Goodbye," the woman said as the door closed behind them.

"Lemuel was right about Ms. Davis," Hillary said as she and Jeff walked down the hall. "She's very serious about her work."

"Just one of the many reasons that people are scared of the IRS," Jeff said. "Let's grab lunch before we go to the bank."

"No," she said. "Let's go to the bank and get home. I'm not very hungry, anyway."

"Do you feel all right?" He slipped his arm around her shoulder and leaned to kiss her forehead.

"I feel edgy, Jeff. That's all." Hillary slipped her arm around Jeff's waist, happy to accept the support of his strong body beside her. "I feel as if I'm missing something. It's like something has happened, or is going to happen, and I'm going to miss it if we don't get back soon. Let's go to the bank and get it over with."

"Sure. I'd like to get back, too."

Jeff couldn't help but notice the nervous movement of her eyes when she spoke of going home. Before their talk with the IRS agent, she'd been happy. Actually, she'd been downright ebullient. Even after their disappointing interview, she'd been upbeat, though angry. Now, however, at the mention of home, she seemed to be struck by a wave of anxiety.

He wondered if she would ever feel at home in her Napa Valley house again, but he didn't ask her. He wanted to protect her and to keep her mind at ease. To that end, it seemed best not to dwell on the matter of her recent troubles and give her time to recover.

Certainly the best thing for Hillary was for the mystery of Albert's death to be solved as soon as possible. They were certainly in agreement about that. So they hurried to the bank.

"I'm sorry to hear about his death," branch manager Arvid Cromwell said after they'd seated themselves in his office. "I don't have any information about Albert's account with us, but I've someone who is bringing us a printout. As I'm quite satisfied with your credentials, I don't mind discussing it. I can't release any money, though, not until I'm officially notified about his death."

"That's quite all right," Hillary assured him. "We just want to get some idea about what he used the account for. To tell you the truth, I had no idea that he had a bank account of any kind in San Francisco."

"That's not entirely odd," the smiling manager said. "Many people keep a variety of bank accounts. I've always seen it as an eccentricity, but in the case of large deposits it's not a bad idea to keep more than one account. That way a person can...ah, here we are."

A young woman had knocked and entered, carrying a sheet of green-and-white striped computer paper; the log of Albert's account use was printed on it.

"Let's see," he said, sitting and squinting down at the paper. "It's a regular checking account. He opened it last December with an initial balance of five hundred dollars. Currently, there is a balance of twenty-five dollars and thirteen cents in the account."

"From five hundred down to twenty-five," Hillary mused. "Did he write many checks?"

"No, not many. They were large ones, though."

"How large?" Hillary asked, afraid to hear the answer even as she asked.

"Several thousand, usually."

"Who were the checks written out to?"

"That's not listed here, I'm afraid," he said, shrugging. "You'd have to look at the returned checks for that."

"I'm afraid we can't do that," Hillary said sadly. "We had a fire the night Albert died. His checking information was burned."

"What was the most that Albert had in the account?" Jeff asked.

"Let's see." The man scanned down the listing, running his thumb down the row of numbers. "The account contained two-hundred-and-sixty thousand dollars in June," he said. "Is that important?"

"We're trying to get a handle on Albert's last weeks," Jeff said. *Two-hundred-and-sixty thousand dollars? What was Albert up to?*

"What about the checks that came through for this month," Hillary said quickly. "Do you still have them?"

"Certainly." He stood and smiled. "Let me see about that for you."

"What was he doing with all that money?" Hillary asked Jeff, when the manager had left the office. "I don't understand it."

"That may be where the loan from Bernard went," Jeff suggested. "But it doesn't explain why he wanted it."

"No, it doesn't explain anything at all."

The banker's return cut off their conversation. He sat behind his desk again, a single check in his hand.

"There's only one check for that account," he said. "Quite a sizable one, too."

"May I?" Hillary reached for the check, taking it across to read the amount. "Fifty thousand dollars? What is this place? The Golden Gate Recovery Project."

"It's a charitable foundation," the man said easily. "They work with the homeless in the area."

"So, it's legitimate?" Jeff asked, leaning to look at the check Hillary was holding.

"Oh, yes, absolutely. Your cousin was apparently quite altruistic."

"Yes, I'm sure he was," Hillary said. "But I find it hard to believe that he set up a secret checking account merely to make charitable donations."

"No, that wouldn't make very much sense," the banker admitted. "Would you like the address of the project? It's right on Market Street not far from here."

"Yes, please." Hillary spoke absently, trying to imagine what Albert was thinking of when he opened this account. That was beyond her imagination.

"There you go," the banker said, sliding a slip of paper with the address across to her. "Is there anything else I can help you with today?"

"No, that's all." Hillary sat for another moment thinking that she would never see a reason for Albert's strange behavior. Only when Jeff stood beside her did she stand and nod toward the bank official. "Thank you for your time," she said. "We'll contact you about the account later."

"That would be fine," he said, walking with them to the door. "And please accept my condolences on your loss."

"Thank you," she said again. "Goodbye."

The mystery was not becoming any more clear with scrutiny. If anything, it was all becoming more obtuse. Would they ever know what happened to Albert?

THE GOLDEN GATE RECOVERY Project was based in a small second-floor office downtown. The two rooms the establishment occupied in the old building were clean, newly painted, and the used furniture showed their frugality as well as the seriousness of their purpose.

The project workers ran the gamut of ages and, judging by clothing, of social strata. All were going about their duties with an energy that spoke of a great dedication to their work. Hillary and Jeff were directed to a large, smiling woman named Janet Proust, the project director.

"Oh, goodness, I'm so glad to meet you," she said when they'd introduced themselves. "Albert never speaks about himself, so I didn't know anything about his background. It's lovely to meet a member of his family."

"Yes, I—" Hillary couldn't continue. It seemed so heartless to bring grief to this happy woman and add that extra burden to this busy place. It was obvious that Albert was a special friend to those assembled here; Hillary didn't think it was only because Albert had money.

"We have some bad news, I'm afraid," Jeff said, stepping forward. "Albert is dead, Ms. Proust. It happened a couple days ago."

"Dead?" The woman's face fell, utter shock replacing her smile. "But he wasn't ill, was he? I would have thought him to be in the pink of health."

"Yes, but he was murdered." There was no tactful way to put it, and Jeff felt strangely awkward talking to a stranger like this about his late friend. Albert's friendship with Janet Proust seemed strange, too. Jeff had always thought he'd known all of Albert's friends. It was unsettling to find that people had lives beyond your sight, but, under these circumstances, it was even more awkward.

"Murdered?" she asked. "What, a mugging?"

"No, he was killed in his home in the valley. Shot to death."

"My God! That's horrible! Do you know who did it?"

"No, we really have no clue," Hillary said now. "That's partly what brings us here today. We're trying to get a line on Albert's last months."

"Last months? How... what do you mean?" Ms. Proust ushered them through to a second, smaller room as she spoke. "I'll surely help in any way I can."

"It's a bit awkward to explain, I'm afraid," Hillary said, taking the chair the large woman offered to her. "You see, we had no idea that Albert was helping you financially. I work in New York while my cousin worked here at our winery, and I didn't realize that he was spending as much time in the city as he was. Now that he's dead, I think it may be important to find out as much as we can about the time he spent here."

"Certainly." The woman smiled again, but only slightly. "I think what you're avoiding saying is that you weren't kept up-to-date on how much money he donated to us."

"Yes, that's one of the things we don't understand," Hillary admitted. "Some of our financial records were burned, and I don't have a complete accounting. Do you mind telling us how much he gave you?"

"Not at all, dear. It is tax deductible, after all, and you should have a record." She turned her chair toward the desk behind her and typed Albert's name into her computer. "Including his last check, he donated one-hundred-and-thirty-two thousand dollars to the project."

"One-hundred-and-thirty-two thousand?" Jeff couldn't help the shock that registered in his voice.

"Is there something wrong with the donation? Wasn't the money his to give?"

"Oh, yes, it was his," Hillary said quickly. "I have no problem with the donation. I just didn't know how much it came to."

"Are you sure you're telling me all there is to know?" She swung her chair around again, studying Hillary and Jeff closely. "I do social work here, you understand. I'm used to people trying to conceal things from time to time, and I'd say that you're holding something back."

"Yes, we are," Hillary said. "I just don't know if it's proper to tell you all of it."

"Maybe not," Ms. Proust said. "But Albert came here off and on since Christmas. He didn't just give money but time, as well. Whether he was serving food at the lunch counter or handing out blankets at the shelter, he was a good worker. A real friend to us. I'm only sorry we didn't see him more often than we did, and not just because he was a good worker, but because he was a genuinely nice man. I liked him."

"Yes, he was a very nice man."

Hillary was suddenly on the verge of tears. This reminder of her cousin's generosity and kindness brought up images of all she would miss about him. No, she couldn't darken this woman's image of Albert with talk of gambling. It was best that someone remember him for only the good things.

"How often did he come in?" Hillary asked, forcing a smile to her lips. "And when did he first come?"

"The first time was just a couple days before Christmas. He walked in off the street and wrote us a check for ten thousand dollars and walked out again. He didn't even introduce himself that first time.''

"Isn't that a bit odd?" Jeff couldn't see any pattern in Albert's activities so far, and this wasn't helping discern one.

"It's not odd for people to drop off money quickly like that. Some people prefer to do their charitable work on the run, so to speak. But for a donation of that size, people usually wait for a receipt."

"Did you try to find out anything about him then?"

"No. We're busy enough most times, but Christmas is pretty hectic. To tell you the truth, I didn't expect the check to clear the bank. It did, though, that very afternoon."

"When did he come in again?" Hillary asked.

"After the New Year. This time he came in and talked with some of our volunteers. I didn't recognize him at first since he was here so briefly the first time. When I did get his name, I made sure that he accepted the receipt for his donation. He didn't seem to care much about keeping a record of it, though."

"Why?"

"I don't know," the woman said thoughtfully. "He acted as though he felt that claiming it as a deduction would cheapen the gift in some way."

"Did he make another donation that time?"

"No, but he volunteered to help us. As I recall, he helped at the lunch counter for the next two days. He didn't make another donation for a month or so, and I never asked for one. After all, ten thousand from one person is quite a gift." She nodded, smiling.

"Did you notice anything strange about his behavior?" Hillary asked. "Aside from his attitude about money, did he act nervous or unusual in any way?"

"No, he was as calm and levelheaded as anyone could hope to be. He did suffer from migraines, though. He had a terrible headache one afternoon that nearly had him in tears."

"Albert didn't have migraines," Hillary said, more to herself than either of the others.

"That's what he said they were, anyway," Ms. Proust volunteered.

"He never acted nervous about anything?" Jeff asked.

"No, except about the lottery, of course. But I don't think I'd call that nervous, really. Excited, I guess."

"About the lottery?"

"Yes. There too, though, I don't think he cared so much about the money as he did about winning."

"Why don't you think he cared about the money?"

"On the second day he worked with us he brought in a whole bunch of lottery tickets. He just passed them out to everyone who was handy and wished them all good luck. It was like watching a kid at Christmas. Nobody won, of course, but it was fun, anyway."

"Did he give away lottery tickets often?"

"Not often. A couple more times as I recall. Is that important?"

"Not that I know of," Hillary said. "He didn't ever mention any people? A man named Winger, for instance? Maybe a man named Foche?"

"No, he never spoke about anybody. As I said, I didn't even know about Albert's family."

"That's about all we have to ask you," Hillary said, standing quickly. "I'm glad that Albert was able to help you out."

"Help us! Why he paid off our equipment, paid for food for most of the year, and paid a couple months of rent in the bargain. Your cousin was a saint. An honest to God saint."

Chapter Twelve

"Will the real Albert de Gaetano please stand up," Hillary said sourly as they began their drive out of the city. "He was either a saint or an uncontrolled gambler or what? What else is there to find out about Albert?"

"Don't ask me," Jeff said. "I'm still not sure they're talking about the same man I grew up with. This is all too weird."

"He didn't have migraines, though, I know that. God, Jeff, I was here for Christmas and he didn't say a word about that donation. Not one word."

"Maybe he thought you'd object."

"Why would I object? Because we couldn't afford it? We could then. Now, however, I'm not sure if we could afford to be so magnanimous. Not the way he went through money, we can't."

"How do you stand now?"

"I don't know," she admitted, clenching her fists on the wheel. "The books I had show that everything is just fine. But that can't be true, because Albert couldn't have supported this kind of living from his personal account."

"Are you sure?"

"If I can't, then he couldn't," she said positively. "He spent two-hundred-and-sixty thousand dollars from one account that we know of. Now I wouldn't doubt that his gambling debts were every bit as high as his donations, even if Winger wouldn't be specific. And we don't know if he donated elsewhere, either. I'm going to have to go to his other bank in the morning, and I don't think I'm going to enjoy the visit."

"How are you holding up?" Jeff massaged the back of her neck, wishing she'd at least let him drive so he could feel useful again. Now that he felt sure of his standing with her, he wanted to do as much as he could for her.

"I'll live," she said. Then she smiled, glancing his way coquettishly. "Maybe we can relax together when we get to my place," she said. "You can give me a proper massage."

"You've got it," he said. "There's nothing like a full body massage to relax a person after a hard day."

"It had better be a good one to drive this day out of my mind," she said. "Boy, Jeff, Albert had never been so busy as he was these last seven or eight months. No wonder he made so many trips to San Francisco."

"There's probably a logical explanation. Something that ties all these events together."

"Sure there is," she said ruefully. "My cousin was insane. That's the only answer I can come up with. He was certifiably nuts."

They drove north as the shadows lengthened in the growing sunset, slowly leaving the urban surroundings for the grassy hills of the countryside. The vineyards grew more plentiful around them as they passed signs that advertised the wine country tours.

Hillary drove resolutely, increasing their speed as they drew closer to their destination. She had to get home as soon as possible. Home, the one place where a bit of sanity still remained. Or did it? Whatever the case, Jeff had become her primary source of sanity. Without him and the shelter of his love, she felt that she might go crazy. Now she wanted to leave the questions about Albert behind her and give herself to his love once more.

Only Jeff's love could remind her that she still had a future, for everything else in her life seemed to have come to an end.

HE WATCHED THEM DRIVING along the road to Hillary's house. They'd been together, he could sense it. They had consummated their relationship, and that angered him beyond words. If he could only strike now, he'd kill them both. He'd ignite the wiring in their motor carriage as he'd done with the office and burn them to cinders. That's what he'd do if he could strike at this instant, for she'd betrayed him. She'd made a fool of him again.

But his love was greater than any momentary anger, and he fought with the impulse to make her pay. Both his love and his desire for revenge stopped him. He didn't dare do anything to either of them until Bernard Foche had paid his debts. He was the one who was due punishment, after all, not her.

Not Marie.

She didn't know, after all. He couldn't punish her for not knowing. And he didn't want to kill Jeff, not if he could help it, anyway. If it came down to it, however, he would do what he had to do.

Tomorrow, he would do something to get the boy out of the way. For now, he would take her from Jeff tonight, before they could be together again. This time, once he had her, he would keep her.

This time, she wouldn't get free. She'd come with him forever.

If she refused to come with him? He couldn't believe she would refuse. But if she did, he would punish her, along with Foche.

THE CLOUDS HAD GATHERED into a black mass overhead by the time they reached Hillary's house, and the slight smell of dampness in the air foretold of coming rain. Hillary stopped the car in front of the house and closed her eyes. She felt suddenly tired. She rolled her shoulders to rid herself of the kinks that had settled into her muscles. She would love a hot bath and a meal, would love to watch the rain bathe her vineyards with health-giving moisture. And she would truly love to be alone with Jeff all through the night. But she knew now that she wasn't going to do any of those things. She was too tired to even attempt them.

"You're dead tired, aren't you?" Jeff stroked her shoulder, smiling with total devotion. "Should I go home?"

"Oh, Jeff, I don't want you to leave," she said feebly, as she removed the keys from the ignition. He was so handsome, sitting there patiently, without demand or expectation, that she wanted to smother him with the full effect of the love that had bloomed in her heart.

"You're going to fall asleep here if we sit too long," he said, stroking her cheek. "Let me tuck you in, and I'll be on my way."

"I'll miss you if you go," she said.

"No, you'll be sleeping before I'm out the door." Jeff threw his door open and got out. The blustering wind mussed his hair like mischievous fingers. He walked around and helped her from the car. "Come on."

"Do you mind?" she asked. She felt almost foolish. How could she be this tired when she'd looked forward to so much on the drive back?

"I don't mind." Taking her hand in his, Jeff led her toward the house. "We've got other nights."

"God, I'm tired."

Hillary allowed Jeff to unlock her door. She walked automatically to her bedroom and switched on the light. Jeff followed, pausing at her door as she turned back the covers.

"Will you be all right?"

"Yes. I just need a night's sleep and I'll be just fine."

Heedless of him watching her, she unbuttoned her blouse, removed it and slipped out of her shoes and slacks before sitting on the bed. Once seated, she had no further desire to prepare for bed, only to lie on it. And, once she lay down, she was asleep.

Jeff chuckled quietly, then he stepped in to remove her knee socks and slip her legs beneath the bedding. Snuggling her blanket securely beneath her chin, he bent and kissed her cheek. "Good night, beautiful Hillary," he whispered. "Sweet dreams."

Hillary smiled in her sleep. She was still smiling when he turned out the lights and left her house.

JEFF HAD NEVER FELT so good in his life. He had expected love to be a mostly physical thing, a need for the heat and the passion of sexuality. But being able to leave Hillary alone without regret made him know that this love was right. This love was forever and would never contain regrets. Any little favor he could do for her would be a further fulfillment of his love.

At this point, he was sure that Hillary planned to move back to the valley, to run the winery. Still, Jeff would gladly sell his paper and move to New York to be with her, if she wanted that. His love for her was so right that nothing else mattered at all.

The cool night wind that bit into him went unheeded as he walked to his car. It didn't matter that he was cold or that it was raining before he'd gotten safely into his vehicle.

When the rain began, it began full force. Heavy sheets of water washed over his windshield as he turned off Hillary's drive and onto the two-lane road leading to town. The vines were taking a beating under the initial assault of the rain, but this force wouldn't last. He could see that the damage would be minimal, especially in light of the dryness that prevailed in the valley. This was a good rain, a necessary rain.

It seemed fitting somehow that it rain tonight. Like the drought that was breaking around him, his long indecision over admitting his feelings to Hillary had ended. And it had ended as he'd never dared to hope. Life was wonderful, and the long drive over the rain-slicked road was as pleasant a drive as he'd ever taken.

Water washed over the roadway, running from the heat-packed earth of the fields in rivulets. His Jeep skidded on a corner, reminding him of the weather and slowing him down from the headlong pace at which he'd begun. There was all the time in the world to get back to town, and he surely didn't want to run off the road. Not now.

He came to a twist in the road where it dropped more steeply from a slow rise near a lone oak tree. To his left, just below the hill, the de Gaetano winery buildings stood hidden by the rolling countryside. Behind him and to his right was the house where his love lay sleeping.

Glancing up as he began the turn, he saw a dark figure standing in the clearing of the vines beneath the oak tree. A man was there, the wind whipping his coat outward like a raven's wings. It was strange how his hat managed to remain firmly on his head in that wind.

For a second, Jeff had the feeling that he knew the man, but he was too far away and the night was too dark. The man just *felt* familiar, somehow, and it was an oddly disquieting feeling to think such a thing.

A spear of lightning leaped from one cloud to the next overhead, illuminating the hilltop briefly. The man was gone. If he'd had time, Jeff would have been struck by the way the man had seemed to disappear. But he didn't have time to think of that.

The man was on the road right in front of him.

He wasn't more than ten yards away, in the middle of Jeff's lane. Jeff reacted instinctively. He jerked the wheel of his car sharply to the left, panic washing coldly through him. The Jeep reacted swiftly, too swiftly, in fact, for it slid on the slick surface of the road. He spun around, fighting the wheel back to the right as he pumped the brakes as lightly as possible. The tire caught the edge of the road, stopped his spin abruptly and threw him against the steering wheel. The car tipped upward, straight off the edge of the road and down the steep incline. It rolled twice before coming to rest on its side at the edge of the sloping vineyard.

Jeff hung suspended against his shoulder harness. He was unconscious, and a trickle of blood flowed from a bump on the left of his forehead where he'd struck the wheel. Behind him, the rain was already washing away the signs of the skidding car.

The dark man stood beside the car and stared through the windshield at the unmoving occupant. Apparently satisfied with his handiwork, he turned and looked up the hill toward the old oak. It was time to go now.

She was waiting for him.

BERNARD FOCHE AWOKE from a fitful sleep to the sound of thunder. He'd been dreaming about the old house, seeing it in flames in a rainstorm with the wind swirling the smoke of the fire into a whirlwind overhead.

Yes, burn it now.

It was the perfect time to get rid of the old rat trap. Lightning would be blamed for the fire and the rain would keep the flames from spreading. Perfect timing.

Bernard got out of bed quickly and dressed in the dark. It wouldn't do to have anyone wondering about his late hours. When he was ready, he let his gray Jaguar glide down the drive and onto the narrow road passing his house before turning on the ignition.

He didn't dare let anyone connect him to this deed.

HILLARY WAS WALKING along the wagon track toward the old barn near the pressing sheds. Her long gingham skirt hung limply around her legs, trapping the August heat beneath it. Her high-necked blouse was no cooler; the white cotton clung to her warm skin. Even as she walked, she couldn't help but marvel at how increasingly realistic her dream became each time she went back to it. She could actually feel the heat. She wondered what Jeff would think of this strangely realistic dream when she told him. There was no way she could adequately describe it to him.

The scenery around her seemed to shrink and flatten in her vision. The colors dimmed slightly as if beginning to drain away, and the heat against her cheeks lessened. She began to see Jeff's face washing in like a watercolor painting against the sky. He was smiling. His face seemed even more real than the valley had appeared moments before. The thought of him was comforting. She heard a sound.

It was the sound of hoofbeats. Jeff's face disappeared. The valley was fully in view again. She felt the heat and the texture of the breeze; the horseman was approaching. This time, however, the sound didn't frighten her. She wanted the rider to approach and turned eagerly to greet him.

The horseman slowed his mount, turning in the saddle as if looking for someone who was following him. After watching for a moment, he turned his horse from the track and into the vineyard.

Hillary's heart sank. He wasn't coming for her! The dark man had other business there, and she was only a spectator to it.

He rode his horse carefully through the vines. A second person emerged from the shadow of the oak on the hill beyond the field. A woman, dressed in much the same clothing as Hillary, was waiting for him by the tree.

Seeing her, the man urged his horse to greater speed, clearing the far edge of the field at a brisk trot. He was impatient, and he jumped from his horse halfway up the hill and ran to the woman who was running down to him. They embraced with a passion that clearly overwhelmed them.

Hillary felt foolish and embarrassed to be watching them like this, but she couldn't turn her gaze away from the two lovers. That was indeed what they were. She could feel the force of their love even at this distance. Finally, they parted enough to run up the hill where Hillary could see a basket. They kissed again before sitting to share the picnic in the cool shadow of the old tree.

Hillary paused, not knowing how to handle the situation. It was her dream, so she felt that she should maintain some control over it. Yet the two people clearly wanted privacy.

She began walking unbidden toward the oak tree on the hill. This dream suddenly seemed to have a will of its own, and Hillary let it take her toward them.

They were lying side by side and looking up at the clouds through the moving leaves of the tree when Hillary reached the crest of the hill. Content to lie in each other's arms, they didn't speak but only smiled and watched the movement of nature around them. Hillary stood behind the tree so their faces were obscured by her angle of view.

She walked to their side without disturbing them and looked down at them. Staring at the two people, Hillary felt suddenly as though someone had struck her with a vision. She was looking at herself and Jeff! Or if it wasn't the two of them, they certainly bore a striking resemblance to them.

But it wasn't Jeff any more than it had ever been Jeff. It was the same man she'd been seeing in her dreams. The woman looked exactly like Hillary, but her eyes were brown and her hair darker.

She didn't know why the sight of them frightened her, but it did. She wanted to turn and run, but she couldn't move. She was rooted to that spot beneath the tree, frozen above them.

But then the man turned his head and looked up at Hillary, his eyes making clear contact with hers. He smiled and nodded in greeting.

"Hello, my love," he said. "I've been waiting for you."

JEFF'S FIRST CONSCIOUS thought was that he should close the window that was letting the draft into his room. It was too cold to sleep.

Then he became aware of the pressure of the harness and of the awkward angle at which his head hung. He opened his eyes and blinked the sight back into them.

The rain had stopped, but the clouds were still thick overhead. The night around him was ominously black, leaving him with nothing but his returning memory and the smell of gasoline to tell him where he was.

When he lifted his head, starbursts flashed within his eyes accompanied by a throbbing pain. The car creaked with his movement. The wind rustled through the vines outside. The smell of gas seemed to grow stronger, compounding his headache.

He had to get out of the ruined vehicle.

Carefully, Jeff pulled his right leg back and angled it down to stand on the passenger door. Then, placing his left foot on the hump in the floor over the drive shaft, he pressed the release button on his seat belt. It wouldn't release at first, so he jammed his thumb against it. He disentangled his arms from the harness and tried to push the door open above him. It was no use. He didn't have the strength to open the door. The window was unbroken, so he cranked it down and grasped the door with both hands, hoping he would at least have the strength to pull himself out before the gas fumes overcame him.

Climbing out of that car was the hardest thing he'd ever done, but he made it. He lay in the mud, gasping in cool moist air while the world seemed to spin beneath him. After a moment, he stood, his head hammering in protest. Trying to ignore the many aches in his back and limbs, he climbed up to the road and began walking toward Hillary's house.

It was his own fault for not paying attention to the road. He should have seen that guy sooner.

Why didn't that jerk help me out? As his memory of the event came back, that was the most important question. *After I went in the ditch to avoid hitting him, the least he could have done was pull me out of the car.*

But the man hadn't helped him and, apparently, hadn't called anyone else to help. He'd simply vanished as quickly as he'd appeared.

Vanished?

Then he remembered how the man on the hill had disappeared. And he remembered how the man on the road had been dressed. He'd been wearing a black coat and hat with a white shirt and bolo tie. If Jeff wasn't sure it was a crazy idea, he'd swear he'd seen the same man whom Hillary had imagined.

That isn't possible, is it?

He didn't know what was possible. All he knew was that it was cold and dark and the normally familiar countryside was like a foreign wilderness around him.

It frightened him to be out here alone, and he hastened his step despite the protest of his legs. He wanted to find light and warmth; he wanted to clean up and take account of his injuries.

Eventually, his pace quickened to a limping run. And the faster he ran the more his heart seemed to fill with dread. And, though he was quite conscious of the foolishness of his fear, he couldn't fight it.

Something was behind him. He knew it. Something in the fields was chasing him, rustling the vines with its heavy tread and breathing its cold breath on his neck. Something was back there.

Behind him, Jeff could hear hoofbeats.

BERNARD LIT THE KEROSENE with a wooden match, smiling as the fuel ignited and the flames spread over the old flooring of the bedroom. There were more leaks in the roof than he'd imagined, and he'd been worried that the wet house wouldn't burn, but it seemed to have caught fire well enough. As long as it didn't begin to rain again, the heat of the fire would dry the moisture from the surface of the wood until it could catch at the tinder-dry core. In that way, the house would surely become an inferno.

He paused to glance at the old trunk against the far wall. For a moment, he was tempted to skirt around the flames and look inside the trunk. No, the fire was spreading faster. It would trap him if he tried to reach it.

The important thing to do now was to get away from the area as quickly as possible. There were no immediate neighbors. Hillary's house was three miles away, but she couldn't see the old place from there. Still, he couldn't be sure that someone wouldn't pass on the road and see the flames. He had to be away from the scene of his crime before the flames became too apparent.

Taking his empty kerosene can, Bernard turned and hurried down the steps. He made his way by the glow of the fire behind him and didn't stop until he reached his car.

It was a good night's work. He had parked on the road so that he wouldn't leave tracks in the mud and had kept to the sparse patches of grass when he approached the house to avoid leaving footprints. All in all, Bernard Foche was very well satisfied with his execution of the deed. The evidence would be gone soon. It would be properly buried along with the other dead memories in the old house, and he wouldn't have to worry about anyone finding his secrets.

He had no idea why he'd taken the gun in the first place. Once he had touched it, however, it became imperative that he remove it from Albert's office. And once he'd done that, it had become a threat. Now that threat had been removed. Or it would be when the flames were finished with their work.

He drove home satisfied that he was safe, put his car away and went to bed without a worry left in the world. He was asleep when the rain began again.

JEFF WAS ABOUT A MILE from Hillary's when the rain began falling in icy sheets that took his breath away. It rained so hard that he couldn't see more than a few feet ahead of him, and the force of the water pushed him back a step at first.

He was too tired to run now, so he leaned into the wind and trudged through the rain, clinging to the thought of warmth ahead of him.

He'd stopped running long before the rain, of course. He was too stiff and tired. He'd stopped and turned to look behind him on the road. As expected, he saw nothing but the dark roadway, the hills lit by occasional flashes of lightning. There wasn't anything more threatening than some wet grapes there.

Now he wished he had kept running. He'd be closer to shelter if he had. There was nothing to do now but continue and hope he didn't catch pneumonia. He wondered if he looked as bad as he felt. The last thing he wanted to do was to frighten Hillary by showing up at her door like a refugee from a war in the vineyards. The one good thing about the rain was that it was washing away the blood and grime. At least he'd be a clean refugee.

The ten minutes it took him to walk that last mile seemed like an hour, but at last he was standing in the shelter of Hillary's narrow entry porch, squeezing his hand down into the soggy pocket of his jeans for the key she'd given him.

The rain hadn't lessened its force one bit as he'd walked. At this rate, it would wash everything off the sides of the mountains before it was finished. Where they had fretted about the drought, they'd be reporting flash floods in the next issue of the *Press*. The hard-packed earth wouldn't be able to soak up this deluge.

Jeff slipped the key into the lock and turned the knob, entering quickly. "Hillary!" he shouted. He locked the door behind him. "Hillary!"

Shut up, idiot. She's sleeping.

There was really no point in waking her, so he began getting out of his wet clothes in the front hall as quietly as possible. Every item of wet clothing protested its removal and stuck to cloth and skin with extreme tenacity. When he had finally gotten down to his underwear, he felt like the victor of a wrestling match.

Jeff took his wet clothes around to the laundry room off the kitchen, stuffed everything into the dryer and started it. There was a long blue terry-cloth robe in the guest room, and Jeff snuggled into it gratefully. Now he was beginning to feel human again. He belted the robe tightly around his waist. Only then did he go to tend his wound.

He could hear Hillary moving in her sleep as he used the bathroom outside her door to wash his face and apply a Band-Aid to his forehead. The bruise was a purple lump on the left of his head, but the cut hadn't been bad and a single adhesive strip covered it. He'd live.

Now to get some sleep, he thought. The guest room looked good, but he might oversleep in there. He didn't want to surprise Hillary in the morning by stumbling out of her guest room unannounced. Besides, he wanted to be able to hear when the dryer was finished with its load so that he could get dressed again. Hillary might have callers in the morning, and he'd just as soon be fully clothed if anyone did arrive. With that in mind, he went to the couch.

The buzzer on the dryer woke him later. It was two in the morning, but he got up and dressed, anyway. Before going back to sleep, he went to Hillary's door and listened. She moved slightly, her bed creaking. She was all right. He returned to the couch and lay down with the robe spread over him.

Moments later, he dreamed that he was walking through one of the de Gaetano vineyards. It was the vineyard where he'd crashed his car earlier.

The car was there, in fact, lying on one side just as he'd left it. The road wasn't there, though. In place of the black strip of asphalt, there was a wagon track running through the vines. In front of him stood the old oak tree.

Two people embraced beneath it—a man and a woman. The woman seemed to be struggling, pulling away from the man's insistent arms. And, though he didn't appear to be harming her, the man was obviously not about to let her go.

Jeff wanted to shout at them, but he had no voice. He ran through the vines toward them, seeing them more clearly as he approached. He could tell from his clothing that it was the man he'd seen on the road, but his face looked blank, expressionless.

The woman's back was to him, but she looked familiar. Her blond hair was shining in the hot sun, her long, graceful fingers pushed at the man's shoulders. It had to be . . .

"Hillary!" Jeff's voice returned with the recognition. "Hillary!"

Just as quickly as he shouted her name, the field seemed to lengthen and carry the couple away from him. The grapevines snapped out to snatch at his legs like tentacles. The grasping vines tripped him, and he fell between the vines. He fought to rise, but vines wrapped around his chest and arms. The vines tightened until he couldn't breathe or call out her name. The malevolent vines wrapped his head, covering his mouth and eyes until he was unable to move. They held him there as the sound of Hillary's screams came to him.

He had to get free! He had to get away from those vines!

Jeff awoke when he hit the floor; the robe was wrapped around him, pinning his arms to his body. Shrugging the confining garment off, he lay on the floor for a moment, trying to retain the memory of the nightmare. It had seemed so real that it didn't feel like a dream at all.

But it had only been a dream. After the night he'd had it wasn't surprising that he'd have a nightmare, either. He listened to the rain pouring down outside and relaxed. Maybe it would be better to use the guest room, after all, he thought. The tight space offered by the couch and his impromptu blanket had obviously prompted his dream of being wrapped in vines. If he wanted to sleep at all, he'd better move to a real bed.

He was so tired that he was tempted to stay on the floor. He could sleep here on the warm carpet quite easily. He didn't know he'd fallen asleep again until Hillary's scream woke him moments later.

"Oh, God, no!" she cried. "No!"

Chapter Thirteen

The darkly dressed man kept his eyes on Hillary, holding her transfixed with his gaze even as the scene changed around them. The hill disappeared, the shade of the tree giving way to the hot glare of the sun. He was seated on his horse now many yards away from her. He was too far away for her to see his eyes, but she could feel their possessive gaze. In the irrepressible logic of her dream, she could not move out from under that gaze.

He was riding along the road toward her bringing the recognizable feeling of dread with him. She wanted to run from his path and hide in the vineyard until he passed, but she couldn't move from her spot in the middle of the wagon track. And, as he drew closer to her, she became aware of the sound of a second horse approaching from behind her.

Though she couldn't turn to look at the second horse, she was suddenly aware that the feeling of danger was coming with him, not from the familiar figure who was in front of her. She was afraid of the great hatred that was approaching from behind. She felt a blind rage and she couldn't get out of its way.

Her dream man continued to ride forward at a steady pace. His face, as it became clear, was set in a resolute mask as he prepared to greet the second rider. Hillary felt an overwhelming urge to warn him. He couldn't feel what was coming and couldn't prepare himself for the attack.

Suddenly the hoofbeats grew louder, and a thunderous explosion of sound and movement broke over her as the rider passed through her on the road. He guided his dark horse down the center of the path, riding in a crouch as he bore down on the dream man. Holding the reins in his left hand, his right hung down behind him. He grasped a thick wooden club tightly in his thin fingers.

"Oh, God, no!" Hillary cried now. "No!"

But the rider swung the club in a vicious arc against the other man's head. The blow knocked him from his horse, and he fell like a broken doll in the dirt at the edge of the vineyard.

The attacker wheeled his horse, leaped from the saddle with the club raised in his hand and stood over the fallen man. But he didn't strike again. After a moment, he picked up a large rock from near the path and pressed one side against the blood flowing from the man's head. Then he returned the rock to its place with the bloodied side up and stepped back to examine the scene. After a moment's inspection, he remounted and rode away quickly.

Released from her horrified immobility, Hillary ran to the fallen man and knelt at his side. He looked so like Jeff that for a moment she felt as though it was him who had been so brutally attacked. The thought horrified her, and that horror wouldn't go away even after she assured herself that it wasn't Jeff who lay before her.

She could see that the blow he'd suffered would be fatal. He was still breathing, but in shallow gasps now. "Who are you?" she asked, using the hem of her skirt to wipe the blood away from his face. "Why am I dreaming you?"

"Stay with me," he said with a sigh, trying to lift his hand to touch her. "Stay."

"Don't worry. I'm here," she assured him. "I'm right here."

"Yes," he said, more softly. "Don't leave me, Marie."

"But I'm not Marie."

He didn't hear her. With one last rattling sigh, he was dead.

Hillary found herself crying at the roadside. She didn't know why she was crying unless she was crying for the loss of the perfect love she'd witnessed beneath the oak tree.

But she mourned the loss of this man, as well. She'd been right about him. He wasn't the source of her dread, the other man was. This poor shattered soul had never intended any harm to come to her. He was her friend and he had been trying to warn her, but she'd been unable to warn him on the road.

The sky overhead was darkening now. Time was passing. The body disappeared and the wagon track behind her became a two-lane road paved with asphalt. Hillary stood, surprised to see that she was standing in front of an old house. She couldn't remember why it looked familiar. A man was walking toward the house. Tall and angular, there was no mistaking Bernard Foche's form in silhouette against the moonlit sky. He was carrying something that glittered in the pale light.

As though aware of her watching him, he turned slightly to look over his shoulder. As he did, he moved his burden into full view, and the sight of it chilled Hillary. Bernie Foche was carrying a gun! Albert's gun!

"Hillary! Hillary!" It was Jeff's voice, calling from far away.

No, don't wake me up yet. I have to see what he does.

"Hillary, wake up."

The ground was shaking now, her shoulders moving in an invisible grip.

No, don't wake me!

Bernard emerged from the house. Flames began to lick outward from the upper-floor windows.

"Hillary!"

Her dream dissolved around her, dropping her with a jolt into her dark bedroom. The sound of rain echoed through the air. Above where she lay, she could see the outline of Jeff's anxious face as he continued to shake her carefully but with increasing force.

"Wake up!"

"I'm awake," Hillary said, surprised by the sound of her own voice. "What are you doing here?"

Before he could answer, a flash of lightning illuminated the room. In the harsh light Hillary could see the large bruise that swelled and discolored the left side of Jeff's forehead. For a second, she saw the torn flesh and blood of the wound suffered by her dream man. She saw Jeff dying as surely as the other man had died. The wounds were in identical places.

"Oh, Jeff," she cried, throwing her arms around him and pulling herself up to him. "Oh, Jeff, don't go!"

She held him with the insistence of a woman who had seen how quickly love can be lost. Life was too easily snatched away, and Jeff might be taken in the time it took to swing a club or fire a gun. She couldn't let that happen...couldn't let them be apart again.

"IT WAS SO REAL. I could feel the heat of the sun and the movement of the breeze. And the colors—the colors were so bright and real. It wasn't like a dream at all, Jeff. Not at all."

The coffee was hot and comforting, and in the soft light of her living room, Jeff's injury bore no real comparison to the horrid wound the man had sustained in her dream. Snuggled in her robe and warmly encased in Jeff's comforting arm on the couch, her dream seemed exactly that—a dream, and nothing more.

"You scared me for a moment," Jeff said, waiting for her to say more about the dream. He hadn't completely explained his accident yet, not wanting to say anything about the man unless she brought him up first. "I thought you were being attacked when you called out like that."

"I wasn't, but I remember someone being attacked. There were two men on horseback." But she was having trouble remembering more than that. The dream was fading quickly, leaving only traces of the events.

"There was something important in that dream, Jeff!" she exclaimed, turning in his arm to look at him. "I remember that I didn't want you to wake me because something important was happening. Now I can't remember what it was."

"Don't worry," he said, smoothing her hair back from her face. "It was only a dream."

"No, it wasn't," she insisted. "It was more than a dream. It was a warning. No, more like a message. He was trying to tell me something all along."

"Who was?"

"The man I told you about. The man in the black coat. He told me to come to the Napa Valley for some reason, and it wasn't just because Albert was going to be killed. Now he's trying to tell me something else."

"But you only dreamed him, Hillary. He can't tell you anything."

"Yes, he can, Jeff. Wait, I know." She hurried to where she'd placed the sheet of printout paper she'd brought home from the winery office.

"Here," she said, bringing the paper back to the couch. "I'm sure he sent this poem to me."

"He did? This unnamed spirit sent it?"

"Yes." And as she said it, she was indeed certain of that fact. Somehow, the man was able to reach beyond her dreams to communicate in the real world.

As Jeff took the paper, a cold feeling grew within him. As much as he wanted to remain a skeptic, he couldn't ignore his own experience this very night. He read the sheet again, looking for the clue that Hillary expected was there.

Old houses secret with decay. Old loves smile softly to betray. Old dreams, old fears, never die. And old lovers will never release the living nor abdicate the vigil of their love.

"It's still bad poetry," he said, giving her the sheet as she sat beside him again. "Old loves. Old houses.

Old fears. Everything is old. Other than that, I can't see anything interesting about it.''

''There has to be something.'' Yes, and she could almost see what it was, almost remember the dream from which she'd been awakened.

Hillary closed her eyes now, trying to picture her dream. ''It was old in the dream, too,'' she said softly. ''The old barn was still there and our old house. The road was just a wagon track, and the vineyards weren't nearly so extensive as they are today. I remember that it was hot. Bright sunshine. And then I heard a horse approaching. Yes, he was on horseback.''

At the mention of the horse, Jeff couldn't help but remember his own feeling that a horse had been behind him when he'd left his wrecked vehicle. He remained silent, however, rather than break her concentration on the dream. The more she said, the more he believed that she was right and the less he wanted her to be right.

''You were on horseback. No, not you, but a man who looked like you. He wasn't coming for me. He went to the old oak tree on the hill. A woman was waiting for him,'' Hillary said. ''They kissed. Oh, Jeff, they were so much in love that I felt like a fool watching them. They were in love, but it seemed hopeless, somehow. I don't know why, but it seemed destined not to last.''

''The old oak, you said.'' Jeff cut in briefly, wanting to be certain of the location. ''The one on the hill now?''

''Yes, that's the one. Franz wanted to cut it down and plant there, but Dad wouldn't hear of killing that old tree. Lord knows how old it is. It was pretty big in my dream. Is it important?''

"Go on, and I'll tell you later." He tightened his arm around her shoulder, waiting for her narrative to resume. Outside, rain beat in a constant rhythm.

"I remember walking up to them. I had the impression that they met here regularly, and I think it was a clandestine arrangement. I was looking at them and, and—I don't remember what it was about the two of them . . . Something, but I can't remember now."

"Skip it, then. Maybe it will come to you."

The rain lashed at the window behind them. The storm was kept safely at bay by the glass, but Hillary couldn't help but feel its chill in her bones.

"There were horses," she said now. "Two men on horseback. My man was approaching from the front. I couldn't see the other man until it was too late. He rode right through me!" She spoke faster now, the memories threatening to overwhelm her ability to interpret them. "Oh, Jeff, he had a club in his hand, and he struck the other man—my man—yes, he struck him with the club. He knocked him from his horse, and then he came back and arranged things to make it look like an accident. It was a murder, Jeff! I dreamed about a murder in our vineyards!"

Now that she'd retrieved the dream she couldn't get rid of it. She saw the man lying on the ground again, saw the blood and watched him take his last breath. With tears streaming down her cheeks, she continued talking in a tightly excited voice.

"I'm sure that it looked like an accident to anybody who came along later, but it wasn't. It was murder. God, Jeff, he was so much in love with her, and she with him. They were so perfect together, and he was taken from her, just like she'd been taken from him."

Hillary no longer knew where her words came from, surely not the dream, but she let the words fall, afraid to stop the flow. "She was stolen from him when he was away, you see. Yes, that's what happened. That's why they met in secret. They were planning to marry but he went away. Her name was Marie. She was stolen from him, lured away by promises and lies. And when they found each other again, even those brief moments together were taken away. He was murdered to keep them apart!

"Yes!" Hillary sat quickly, wiping the tears away as she looked eagerly at Jeff. "It was her husband who killed him. That's what happened, Jeff."

"Killed who? Who was it?"

"The man who's been coming to me, Jeff. The man who looked like you…" And then she remembered the hilltop and the faces of the two people. "They looked like us!"

"Sure they did. You gave them familiar faces, that's all."

"No, I . . . yes, maybe that's it." Hillary took a deep breath. That was probably true. There was no other reason for them to have their faces. "Still," she said, "I'm sure of the rest of it. I'm sure that these people are more than a dream and that they were in love."

"How can you be sure?"

"I don't know, but I am." Lightning crackled through the sky outside, highlighting the conviction in her eyes. "Just as I'm sure that he sent that poem. That poem has to mean something, Jeff. It just has to."

"'Old loves' might mean something," he admitted. "But 'old houses' makes no connection that I can think of."

"There has to be something about that poem." Just as there was something more to her dream than she could recall, there was something in the poem. "It must have been torture for him to lose her like that," she said, letting her first thoughts come out.

"For whom?"

"Him, my dream man," she said, settling back in the space within Jeff's arm. "He didn't speak up quickly enough. She became impatient, I suspect, afraid that she'd never have the love she wanted. She was afraid that she was growing older and didn't want to live alone, so she accepted another proposal. He lost her by not saying how he felt in time."

"Like I would have lost you?" Jeff didn't want to talk about dreams anymore. The whole thing was beginning to unnerve him. He wanted to leave the realm of dreaming and concentrate on the world of flesh and blood.

"You wouldn't have lost me, Jeff." Hillary kissed his cheek, enjoying the knowledge that their love wouldn't be lost as so many loves had been lost in time. "If either of us were going to marry someone else we would have spoken about our feelings."

"We were fated to be together," he said.

"That's such a romantic thought. I like it."

"So do I, Hillary," Jeff said softly. "You don't know how much I like that thought."

They sat together without talking for a long time. The only intrusion on their thoughts was the rain beating mercilessly against the roof. The storm seemed to have intensified as they'd been talking. Tomorrow, they'd have to inspect the damage their much-needed rain had brought to the valley, but tonight there was nothing to do but sit comfortably in each other's arms and think of the good days to come. Everything would be all right now that they had their love.

"Why did you ask about the tree?" Hillary's thoughts had brought her back to her dream and Jeff's interest in it.

"It's screwy," he said, wondering how to put it into words. "But I think I saw your ghost man tonight."

"You what?" She turned in his arm, gazing keenly into his introspective eyes. "You saw him?"

"I think I may have. He was standing beneath the old oak. Black coat and hat, white shirt, bolo tie. I couldn't make out his face from the road. He seemed familiar, though."

"That's how he was dressed." Hillary's pulse quickened; at last someone had seen him besides her. "What did he do?"

"He just stood there. Then he disappeared. That's when I saw the man in the middle of the road. That's another crazy thing, Hill," he said. "I think it was the same man. He disappeared from the hilltop and then appeared on the road in front of me."

"No, that couldn't be," Hillary said. "He wouldn't have wanted to harm you."

"I didn't say that he meant any harm. He popped up and I swerved to avoid him. That's all."

"So you believe me now?"

"I guess I do." Jeff grinned, kissing her forehead.

"Was there anything else about him?"

"No, but as I was walking back here in the rain, I thought I heard a horse behind me."

"Really! See, it does mean something!"

"Hold on, Hill, that was probably only thunder. It was storming, you know."

"Yes, of course." She glanced out the window, watching the rain run over the glass. "It looks like it's going to be raining for a month."

"We don't need that much rain. The whole valley will wash away if it keeps up this hard. What about your vines?"

"I think we're safe enough. Most of our fields are fairly level. Except the pinot noir. That's a steep grade."

"Where?"

"The de Gaetano-slash-Foche field," she said, laughing wryly. "I almost hope it does wash away. Better that than to let Bernie get it."

"No, you'll beat him on that. I'll bet we can find a connection between Bernie Foche and James Winger."

"You don't suppose that Bernie rigged Albert's gambling in some way. That may have been why Albert borrowed money without telling me."

"Bernie couldn't have forced Albert to gamble, Hillary. Though I wouldn't put it past him to take advantage of it."

"Yes, he sure would. I wonder why he hasn't mentioned the loan to me yet. That's not like him at all. The Bernie Foche that I know would have been gloating about his good luck whether I was in mourning or not."

"He's waiting until the money is overdue."

"Maybe, though that still wouldn't get the field for him." Driven by a gust of wind, the rain drummed louder against the window behind them. There was something about the rain, but what was it? The rain and Bernie Foche? A vague memory was lingering just beyond Hillary's reach, taunting her with its presence.

"You know," she said, "I don't think he wants the field at all. I think it's just a ploy, a way to get at me. I guess the old family feud isn't done yet."

"You wouldn't dare break with tradition, Hillary. The Foche and de Gaetano squabble is a mainstay here. I don't know why it all started, but it sure has lasted."

Strangely enough, Hillary didn't know how the whole thing had begun, either. There had always been animosity between them, but no one had ever said why. It seemed to center on that one vineyard. At least, that had become the focus of the dispute. Surely it wasn't the cause.

"I wonder how it did begin," Hillary mused. "I know that the families came to the valley at about the same time. We were here a year or so earlier."

"That's why you got the better land." Jeff had written enough historical articles about the valley to know that detail, anyway. "They couldn't hold that against you, though."

"No, they couldn't. I wonder if any of the old family albums could give us a clue. Should we take a look?"

"I'm game."

Jeff stood and followed Hillary to the office. She took the family Bible down from a shelf behind the desk. She was about to open it, but laid it aside in favor of an old picture album on the shelf. A picture might jog her memory more quickly than the names written inside the Bible. She opened the cover and gingerly turned the first pages.

"That's an old family picture," she said, indicating a portrait. The group of people were dressed in their Sunday best and posing before the porch of the original house. "That would be Alberto and Lucia in the center. My great-great grandparents. They had seven kids, so that would be them and their spouses to either side and the various grandchildren in the front.''

''There're only six couples,'' Jeff pointed out. ''Did one of the children die young?''

''Not that I know of. Let's see.'' She ran her finger over the picture, counting the people. ''Yes, four boys and three girls. There's obviously someone missing, but everyone is with their spouse in the picture so I can't tell who it might be.''

''I see you aren't the only fluke in the family, anyway,'' Jeff said. ''Your grandmother was obviously quite blond.''

''Yes. The de Gaetano family came from northern Italy. There're a lot of blond Italians.''

''Strange that none of her daughters were blond.''

None of the women in the old print had light hair, though it would seem that the trait would carry down through someone.

''That is strange,'' she admitted. ''Maybe it's a daughter who is missing.''

''Maybe.''

Hillary turned the pages, passing pictures of early harvests and grape pressings. The wine business had been even more labor-intensive in the past than it was now, and the pictures were filled with men wearing mustaches and suspenders. They posed around vats of fermenting grapes or worked in shirtsleeves picking grapes. Turning another page, Hillary stopped and stared at the house pictured in a small portrait.

''Whose house is that?'' A chill gripped her. She shivered involuntarily. ''I don't recognize it.''

''It's the old Foche place,'' Jeff said. ''You remember it. It's just an old wreck now. People are always after Bernie to tear it down but he's too cheap to have it done."

"No," she said, fighting to control the excitement rising within her. "He's going to burn it down, Jeff. He's going to burn it tonight!"

"What?"

"That was the last part of my dream!" She grasped Jeff's shoulders, laughing. "That's it. I saw him set the house on fire. It wasn't in the past, either, because the road was paved."

"You're not making sense, Hillary. I thought you said—"

"I couldn't remember it before, Jeff, but this is the house I saw. He walked into it in my dream and then it was on fire."

"In the rain?"

"To make it look like a lightning strike. Don't you see? He'll burn it down and nobody will think twice about it. He won't have to worry about the fire spreading, either. It's a perfect night to get rid of the evidence! The evidence," she said again, realizing what that implied as the words came out. "Bernard Foche killed Albert, Jeff!" she exclaimed. "He's burning the house down because the gun is hidden in it. He killed Albert!"

"How can you be sure?"

"Because I saw him take the gun into the house in my dream."

"They don't allow dreams into evidence in court, Hillary."

"No, but they'll accept the gun." Hillary hurried from the room, shouting. "We've got to get there before he has a chance to burn the house. We've got to find the gun!"

Chapter Fourteen

The telephone rang.

"Hello." Bernard Foche pulled the receiver to his ear without rising from bed or turning on the light. He wasn't aware of where he was at first, only of the sound of the rain outside. "Hello," he said again.

"You didn't kill my little gambler, did you?" The voice on the other end of the line was cold and calculating. "Did you, Bernie?"

"What?" Bernard sat up now, looking around him as he rubbed his hand over his head. "Winger? Why are you calling at this time of night?"

"Did you kill him?"

"No, of course not." Bernard stared at the window, finally realizing how hard it was raining. "I'm not a complete idiot."

"Good. Just remember who your friends are when you start coming into money. Remember who makes loans, Bernie."

"I remember. I—I've got to go now," he said, swinging his legs out of bed and standing. "I've got something to do."

Bernard hung up the phone before he heard Winger make any reply, but he did hear a voice as he stumbled across the room to get dressed.

Your fire went out, Foche, the voice said. *The posse is on its way right now. They know all about it.*

THE STEADY DOWNPOUR was whipped into blinding sheets by the swirling wind that came down through the mountains. The rain lashed at the car as Jeff drove from Hillary's to the old Foche homestead. Water ran over the lower portions of the roadway, creating gullies.

"I can't tell how far we are, Hill." Jeff had to shout over the sound of the storm raging above them. "I can hardly see the road most of the time. This isn't a very good time to go calling."

"We have to go now," she insisted, leaning close to him and staring ahead at the watery asphalt. It shimmered briefly in their lights with each beat of the windshield wipers. "Bernie is going to get the gun."

"How can you know that?"

"I just know." Her man had told her, not with words but with a feeling, that their evidence would soon be out of reach if they didn't get it tonight. He was helping her, finally making good on his failed attempts to communicate. He was helping her avenge her cousin.

"I know that if we don't get there fast Bernie will beat us to it," she said. "He's on his way right now. Please hurry."

"I'm trying, but I've already been in one accident tonight. I don't feel up to another one."

Jeff smiled grimly. He knew that she was right, but he wasn't as sure as she that the dream man meant no harm. The spirit he'd seen briefly tonight hadn't been

very helpful. He couldn't put it into words, but he felt
that her benefactor had his own purposes in mind.

Still, the gun had to be found. If Hillary felt that
Bernard was going to dispose of it, Jeff wasn't about
to doubt her. All he could do was to keep his eyes open
and his wits about him when they got there. For now,
however, he had to concentrate on getting them there.
The water was running over the road in heavier streams
now. Soon the movement of water down the hillside
would be strong enough to push Hillary's Mercedes
along with it. He wanted to get to the old house as
much for safety as for the gun.

Lightning crackled directly overhead, the bolt siz-
zling into a tree ahead of them and splitting it nearly in
half. Jeff jammed his foot onto the accelerator, sending the car sliding ahead through a shower of leaves
and small branches. They passed the tree just before
the severed section of trunk crashed down on the road.

"That was lucky," he said, his lips set in a taut line
of determination.

"Somebody wants us to make it," she said, straining forward to see through the rain. *He's helping.
Somehow or other, he's seeing us through this.*

"Here's the turn." Jeff slowed the car. It slipped on
the wet pavement and turned awkwardly onto the
gravel road that joined the main road.

Flashes of lightning illuminated the hilly expanse of
the Foche vineyards on either side of the road. Rain-
water was cutting deeply into the rocky soil, under-
mining the vines and tugging at their roots. The bottom
of the car struck ground as they drove over a deep
trough cut into the roadway. It was obvious that they
weren't going to be driving back over this route. If

they'd left five minutes later, they wouldn't have made it.

"There it is!" Hillary felt relief wash over her as she saw the grove of trees surrounding the house.

A minute later, Jeff parked the car in the relative safety of the oaks. His hands ached from the strain of gripping the wheel, and his head throbbed as he craned his neck to see the house through the storm.

"Come on." Hillary threw her door open and jumped out of the car, slipping on the muddy ground in her haste to get to the old house.

"Wait!" Jeff pushed his door open wearily, his cry drowned out by the howling wind. The rain had turned the ground into a sea of mud, and he could barely stand upright as he got out of the car and followed.

Jeff slipped, falling to one knee on the path to the house. As he rose, a flash of lightning illuminated the rear of Bernard's Jaguar. It was parked halfway down the hill where it had apparently slid from the road. Bernie was already there!

Jeff ran, losing precious time stumbling and sliding in the ooze before he finally reached the house. Set on a level in the hill, the house was now surrounded by water. The flood had already carried away what had remained of a picket fence and was threatening the foundation now. He could see that the insistent flow had carried much of the earth away from the downhill side of the cellar wall, and he thought he could feel the house move when he stepped onto the porch.

"Hillary!" Jeff kept his voice low but insistent when he entered the ancient structure.

He had to pause a moment to adjust his eyes to the darkness. It was even more dim than outside. Water ran and dripped through the ceiling and along the walls, leaking freely down from the upper floors. A stink of mildew seeped in from everywhere. It wouldn't have been a pleasant place on a nice day, but tonight it was horrid. Berating himself now for not keeping up, he ran through to the kitchen in the vain hope that Hillary might have waited for him to join her.

His foot snapped through a floorboard just inside the kitchen door, and he jumped back quickly before chancing his weight on any more of the boards. Even through the smell of rain, he could smell the odor of kerosene lingering in the air. Hillary had been right; Bernard had tried to burn the whole place down.

A board groaned from the weight of footsteps overhead. Jeff turned and bolted for the stairway, running up two at a time in his rush to protect Hillary from the man whom they used to laugh at as kids. Jeff wasn't laughing now, not when the man had proved to be a killer who had nothing to lose by killing again.

Only his speed kept him from falling through the stairs on the way up; the same haste almost undid him once he reached the top.

"Stop!" Hillary cried in alarm as Jeff rushed into the bedroom where he'd heard them moving.

He complied as quickly as possible, but not before he felt a sickening sensation. The floor was crumbling beneath his feet. He spun and jumped back to the wall near the door where he'd entered and then turned, taking quick stock of the situation into which he'd stumbled headlong. The center of the floor appeared to have been burned. The surface of the old wood was charred and had burned through in many places before the deluge had put the flames out.

"Bernard had a little accident with matches," Hillary said, affecting a light tone. She was standing against the wall on the other side of the door, and, like Jeff, she was keeping well back from the center of the floor.

"Yeah," Jeff replied. "Spilled a little kerosene, too, I'd say."

"Accidents do happen, don't they?" Bernard Foche was seated casually on an old wardrobe trunk on the far side of the room. Seemingly quite at ease, he held a gun in his right hand. "I wonder what sort of accident will happen to you?" he mused.

"You can't risk an accident," Hillary said. "It will look too suspicious coming on the heels of Albert's murder."

"You are quite right, Hillary," Bernard said. "So perhaps I should arrange a little suicide scene for the police. That might be better, don't you think?"

"No, I don't think so," Hillary said. Though her tone was still casual, there was a hint of reproach edging her voice that was unmistakable. "You had the loan papers to hold against him, Bernie. Why on earth did you need to do it?"

"Do what, dear girl?" He seemed genuinely perplexed at her question.

"Kill Albert, you idiot!" Jeff cut in harshly. "Why did you kill Albert?"

"I didn't, of course," he said with such sincerity that he left both Hillary and Jeff without a ready reply.

Bernard could see how they'd gotten that impression. He'd taken the gun to escape just such a mistake. But because they knew about the loan, they surely could see that he had no motive. He waited, watching them and waiting for a more positive reply from either one. Perhaps he could avoid killing them if they were willing to understand what had happened.

But as he watched, he found that his two old antag-onists were changing before his eyes. More correctly, Hillary was changing. While he'd been looking at Jeff who stood coiled as though ready to attempt a leap across the ruined floor, Hillary had begun to look like something else—something that wasn't quite Hillary at all. As he watched her now, she changed further. Her raincoat darkened to black and she grew taller and put on a stiff-brimmed black hat.

"If you didn't kill him, why did you take the gun?"

The man who had taken Hillary's place asked the question, speaking with Hillary's voice and with a knowing smirk on his lean face. It appeared to Ber-nard that Jeff had been duplicated in the room, though the one who had taken Hillary's place was shorter and less imposing in stature and he wore a smirking grin.

"Why did you?" he asked again.

"You know damn well why I took the gun," Ber-nard spat out angrily. "You made me! I thought you had done it! I thought you were coming for me! Of course I picked up the gun to defend myself, but that's exactly what you wanted, wasn't it? You wanted my fingerprints on the gun, didn't you?"

"What are you talking about?" Jeff spoke cau-tiously. Bernard had lost his casual demeanor and was staring at Hillary now as though he'd never seen her before. More than that, he seemed threatened by her. He was threatened enough that he moved the gun to cover her exclusively. "We weren't there."

"Yes you were," Bernard insisted. "You were there. You told me that you knew about the loan, as well. That's why I can't let you go now."

"What about the loan?" Hillary asked. Had Ber-nard gone mad?

She felt her heart racing as Bernard pointed the gun toward her, his unsteady hand wavering slightly. When she'd first stumbled upon him in the room, he'd smiled and greeted her as though there was nothing out of the ordinary about both of them being there. He'd had the gun then, too, of course. But he'd held it in an unthreatening manner. But something had changed now and he seemed on the verge of firing each time the gun bobbed in his twitching hand.

"What about the loan?" she repeated, hoping to calm him with talk until they could think of some way to get out of this predicament.

Bernard didn't say anything at first, opening his mouth only to close it again in confusion. But Hillary heard another voice speaking close to her ear. "Don't worry," it said. "I won't let you down, Marie. I won't lose you."

She felt encouraged by her dream man's presence in the room, knowing that somehow she and Jeff would get out of this alive. Encouraged, but not safe yet.

"Please, Bernie," Jeff said, watching the gun and measuring the distance across the burned part of the floor. "Tell us what you're talking about. We weren't there."

"You weren't, but he was," Bernard said, still pointing the gun at Hillary. "Once my fingerprints were on the gun, he laughed and said that he knew all about the loan. It was only a matter of time, he said."

It was only as Bernard spoke that he fully remembered the night in Albert's office. The past days, Bernie had lived with a blank space in his memory, doing things without fully knowing why he did them and wondering what was wrong. Now he knew. That man had done something to him to make him forget. The man hoped that Bernie would make a mistake and get caught. He should have shot him that night while he had a chance.

"He knew about Winger," Bernie added, nodding as he came to his decision. "Knew about the forgery."

"You forged the signature on the loan papers?" Hillary asked. "Winger forged them?"

"You know he did!" Bernie shouted at the man who stood where Hillary had been. "You were there! How was I to know that Albert would kill himself? How could I have known that?"

"Kill himself?" Hillary gasped in shock.

"Yes, he—"

Bernard was cut off by a violent shaking of the house and the sound of timbers falling beneath them. Jeff and Hillary stood pressed against their respective walls, but they knew that wouldn't save them.

"The foundation is going!" Jeff called out. "We've got to get out of here!"

"No!" Bernard called. "I can't let you leave. You'll turn me in to the police."

"No we won't," Hillary said. "You didn't kill Albert, and nobody but Jeff and I know about the loan. We can work something out."

"No, we can't," Bernard insisted. "I can't do it any longer, and you know it. Lording that land over us all these years! That damn field! It was ours, dammit! It was to be in the dowry! You owe it to us. To me! The land or the money. You owe me."

The house shook again. The floor began to slant, and a gap opened in the ceiling above them to admit the first feeble light of dawn fighting through the storm clouds.

Jeff looked at Hillary, hoping there was a way to distract Bernard long enough for her to get through the door to safety. As he looked at her, for only a moment, he saw a man in a dark coat and hat in her place. The man seemed to be taunting Bernard, but that couldn't be correct. He wouldn't want to provoke Bernie to fire! Then the vision was gone, and Hillary was looking into Bernie's eyes with determination steeling her gaze.

It was now or never. Bernard could see that the house would topple within minutes and he'd lose his shot at the taunting man in black. With a ragged cry, he raised the gun.

Jeff took a desperate step and jumped at the same time, flinging himself between Hillary and the gun with a shout equal to Bernard's in its agonized fury.

Hillary ducked instinctively as the gun fired. Glancing up, she could see that Jeff had been shot. As she ducked again she saw the dark figure of a man flying toward Jeff. Jeff's feet landed short of safety and broke through the burned wood. The man seemed to push Jeff's body, lifting and propelling him the rest of the way toward Bernard by the far wall. Jeff and Bernie slammed into the wall together. The gun went off again before hitting the floor and clattering away from them.

Then, in a moment of illumination from the lightning overhead, Hillary clearly saw the figure of the darkly dressed man clutch Bernard's coat by the lapels and lift him overhead with a look of hatred on his face. He threw Bernard down through the charred floor.

Hillary's heart froze at the sound of Bernard's cry as he crashed through the floor and through the rotten kitchen floor below to continue down into the cellar.

Then there was a moment of silence before the next rolling crash of thunder, and Hillary raised her eyes to look at the man across the room from her.

It was Jeff, standing dazed at the edge of the ruined floor and looking to her for some explanation of what had happened. The other man was gone. Jeff's leg was bleeding.

The house shifted again, swaying with a sharp snapping sound.

"The window!" Jeff shouted. He held his leg and edged toward the canted space gaping toward safety. "Hurry!"

Hillary stuck to the wall and hurried around to join him at the window overlooking the back porch. Beyond the short roof of the porch a sea of mud was flowing away, carrying debris downhill with it. They had no time to discuss whether or not to join that flow; the house was shivering steadily now and leaning farther over with each jolt.

Hillary climbed onto the roof, gripping Jeff's hands tightly as she lay on her stomach facing him, and felt for the edge with her toes. "Let go," she said, holding herself as flat as possible. He released her, and she let herself slide as quickly as possible to the edge. She had only a moment to glance below her before pushing off and plunging to the flooded yard.

The muddy water was at least three-feet deep where she fell, and the torrent swept her several yards down the slope before she grasped the trunk of a tree and stopped herself. Moments later, Jeff slipped along with the water toward her and gained safety at her side.

"We've got to move! The house will go soon and the debris will all come this way!"

Using trees for support, they made their way out of the deepest part of the flood and regained the high ground near the car.

From there, they could see that the water had entered the cellar through one window and had been flowing through and out a window on the lower side of the slope. The raging waters had made short work of the old mortar holding the stones of the foundation together. It had washed through the lower foundation wall and taken most of the supporting earth away with it, leaving the old house standing on three unstable foundation walls that were now in the process of giving way.

Jeff held Hillary to him fiercely. Their kisses consumed them for the moment, each hungry to confirm their safety in each other's arms.

"I thought he was going to shoot you, Hill," Jeff said, feeling the strength flood out of him now as he spoke. He was feeling light-headed, dizzy now, and found himself holding her as much for support as in loving relief. "God, I feel terrible."

The blood from his wound stained his right trouser leg. The dark color of the blood had begun to show on the wet fabric even while the rain washed it away.

"Here, let me get you into the car," Hillary said.

"Wait," he said. "Look."

Hillary turned in time to see the house give way to nature at last. Falling with a twisting motion, it toppled into the flood running down through the yard, pieces of it breaking free to wash into the vineyards below them. The old house was gone.

"Come on," she said, turning him gently toward her car. "Let's look at that leg."

"That's what I get for playing junior G-man." He laughed, hopping with her to the car. "I don't know how I made that jump."

"I saw it," she said, opening the rear door. "He did it, Jeff. It looked like he flew into you and pushed you across."

"Really? Why did he do that? He's *your* friendly ghost."

"I don't know, but I saw him. He pushed you across and then he . . . he threw Bernie through the floor."

"You saw him do that?" He sat on the edge of the seat, his leg beginning to throb now that the frantic flood of adrenaline had left him. "I don't remember what happened after I jumped."

"Yes, I saw it."

"I thought I saw him, too," he said. "I looked at you and he was—oh, Hillary, I'd better lie down before I fall down."

"Yes, darling," she said, easing him down on the seat. "You rest and I'll get help. Everything is over now."

As she dialed her car phone, she wondered if everything was indeed over. The look on the man's face when he'd lifted Bernard Foche was frightening. It had left her with a feeling of foreboding quite unlike what she'd had before. Now she was afraid for her own life!

HILLARY COULDN'T SHAKE the feeling of being watched throughout the rest of the morning, not even when she reached the hospital. All the while she was waiting for the police to arrive with their four-wheel vehicle she'd felt the eyes upon her, felt those terrible inquisitive eyes. She could even feel their scrutiny now, while sitting at Jeff's side after they'd examined and sedated him. It was as if someone was following her and wanted her to know it. It was as if he wanted her to be afraid.

Of course that was foolishness and she knew it. The man had saved them both that morning. But the look in his eyes haunted her. That horrible look of hatred and triumph was what she couldn't shake.

Hillary hadn't told anyone about the man. She had no idea of how to begin. She had no explanations, no reasons for his arrival or for the dreams he brought with him, and she wasn't about to start spouting off about ghosts and such without some kind of proof.

Was he a ghost? That would seem to be the most logical explanation. The man had been there, after all. She herself had seen him propel Jeff across the burned-out floor. And she'd seen him throw Bernard Foche through the same floor. He had been there.

Hillary decided that she wouldn't tell anyone about it until she'd spoken with Jeff. She wasn't about to link Bernie's death to a ghost sighting without consulting Jeff about it.

She'd never had to talk to anyone about personal decisions before. Anything she did with her life outside of business had always been her own concern and no one else's. Now, however, she had someone involved with her personal life. She had a man to confide in and consult whose opinion could rightly help to guide her decisions. Now she had someone to love, and she liked that idea quite a bit.

Jeff had been lucky. The bullet had gone through his upper leg, damaging muscle and causing substantial bleeding, but it wouldn't result in any permanent disability. They'd sedated him primarily to be sure he wouldn't check himself out of the hospital and go to work.

There was quite a lot of work to do, of course. Hillary's vines had survived the flooding quite well due to their work over the years to provide channels for flood waters to run past the fields. Many other vineyards hadn't been so lucky. The Foche vines had suffered terribly.

Bernie Foche. Only now, hours after their rescue, could Hillary take time to contemplate him and what had happened to them in the storm. She still didn't know why he'd begun to threaten her with the gun. According to him, it was only a matter of forgery. And, though she had no doubt that he was the one who had called the IRS, that wasn't anything they couldn't have worked out. Hillary had paid her debts and she intended to pay Albert's. Bernie didn't have to kill her. Nor did he have to die.

The look in that man's eyes had been so terrible! His was a hatred that seemed to reside deep in his soul; it hadn't been an emotion born of that moment. He had looked victorious. That was the look that scared Hillary now.

The matter of Albert's death was still up in the air, though Hillary was inclined to believe Bernard's statement that he hadn't committed the crime. Was it really suicide? She had no idea.

JEFF AWOKE AGAIN SHORTLY before noon, and Hillary was there to greet him with a kiss that renewed both of their flagging energies.

"I've got to get out of this place," he said, sitting up and scanning the room for his clothing.

"Gil is out covering the flood," Hillary assured him. "And your clothing isn't here, anyway. Just relax and recuperate and let the world get on without you for a day or so."

"Well, I guess I don't feel all that lively, anyway." He settled back with a smile, letting his eyes roam over Hillary as she sat on the bed beside him. "What about Bernie? Is he . . ."

"Yes." She nodded sadly. "They found his body in the rubble. It's a shame, Jeff. And the worst part of it is that I don't know what he was talking about. That stuff about a dowry made no sense."

"I think Bernie was nuts at the end," Jeff offered. But he couldn't help feeling that the statement missed the mark in some way. "Do you think he was lying about Albert?"

"No, I don't," she admitted. "He didn't kill him. After all, he had no reason to kill him."

"What about the suicide? It would fit the physical evidence."

"I know, and that bothers me," she said simply. She didn't want to allow even a possibility of suicide.

"If I had blown a few hundred grand on gambling I might be likely to think of suicide," Jeff commented, more to himself than to her. "Except, of course, that Albert was always one of the least suicidal people I knew."

"Yes, but he wasn't an out of control gambler, either. I'm beginning to think that Albert was the one who was nuts, Jeff. Not Bernie. Not even me."

"Oh, but you definitely are crazy," he said, taking her hand firmly in his. "I mean, to hang out with a guy like me you must be."

"Must be, and I don't expect to be cured any time soon, either." Hillary laughed, squeezing his hand in return. It felt fabulous to have him to herself like this. Retaining the easy friendship and gaining the love, her life was on its way toward being perfect, and all she had to do now was let it happen. "But that wasn't what I meant."

"You're not crazy because you saw the man. I saw him twice, after all."

"Thank God I have a witness. Do you think we should tell anyone about him?"

"Not on your life! I don't want to end up on the cover of the tabloids next to the Hollywood divorces and Bigfoot sightings!"

"Then it will be our little secret." She leaned to kiss him, stroking his hair back from his forehead. "Sealed with a kiss."

"Hey, have you two got some news for the society page?" Gil Dickinson spoke up more to warn them of his entry than to make conversation. He walked into the room and looked down at Jeff with a frown. "You're setting a damn poor example for the staff, lying in bed like this."

"I'd better be the only one relaxing," Jeff shot back, smiling. "Have you got things covered?"

"Yes, I have." The older man placed a hand on Hillary's shoulder, regarding her kindly. "I was sent here to get you," he said. "Chief McDonald has the autopsy results. He wants to talk to you before releasing them to the press."

"My goodness," she said, standing. "Oh, I'd better go Jeff. You stay put now."

"He'll stay," Gil assured her. "You go now. I can't finish my work until the chief gives out his information. Get!"

"Hang in there, Hillary," Jeff commanded as he released her hand. "Remember, anything is better than not knowing."

"I'll try to remember that."

Their eyes met for a moment. Then, with a quick nod, Hillary left the room.

"You feeling all right?" Gil asked, pulling the chair up to sit next to his employer.

"Not too bad, all things considered. How bad are things out there?"

"Foche got the worst of it. But then he never did anything to channel runoff water, anyway. All the storm did was cause erosion more quickly than normal rainfall would."

"What about the de Gaetano land?"

"No problems that I know of. Their field foreman told me they came through just fine. White Horse Winery took some structural damage in their sheds, and a couple others lost some vines. The only heavy flooding was what went through Foche's place. That's strange, too, when you think about it."

"Yes, it is," Jeff said. But it wasn't nearly as strange as the rest of what took place last night.

"Jeff," Gil said, leaning toward the bed. "I want to ask you a stupid question, but I expect a serious answer."

"I'll try."

"Do you believe in ghosts?" Gil asked.

For a moment, Jeff wasn't sure he'd heard the man correctly. He paused a moment to consider his answer carefully. There was no sense in lying to Gil, but if he said too much, Gil might want to make a big deal about it. It was an interesting story, after all.

"Yes, I do believe in ghosts," he said at last.

"That's a shock," Gil said, though a smile warmed his craggy features. "I wouldn't have expected you to believe in stuff like that."

"I've given it some thought lately, and I've come to believe. Why did you ask?"

"That's the stupid part of it." Gil paused, twisting his lips up in an embarrassed smile. "The fact is that I saw one the other night. Think I did, anyway."

"Where?" Jeff wished he hadn't asked so quickly; Gil's eyes sharpened at his response.

"At Albert's place," he said. "You and Hillary were out of town and I wanted to check on something."

"And you broke in," Jeff concluded.

"Right. Hell, Jeff, I knew the cops wouldn't let me in and I didn't know when you'd be back to get permission. I didn't really expect Hillary to mind."

"No, I don't suppose she would. What about the ghost?"

"He chased me out of the house. It scared me to death."

"Chased you out?"

"Sure did. It was like he was protecting Albert's things from intruders."

"You're sure about this?"

"Absolutely. The funny thing was that he looked quite a bit like you."

"Yeah," Jeff said absently. "So I've heard."

"What?"

"No, I'll tell you some other time. For now, let's just say that we're not going to print any ghost stories in our newspaper. Right?"

"I wasn't planning on writing any," Gil stated. "I'd rather continue being able to look people in the eye than do that."

Chapter Fifteen

Chief McDonald was seated in the conference room with another man when Hillary entered. She regarded them self-consciously, aware of her unkempt condition. The chief looked a bit worse for wear, too. His uniform was wrinkled and stained with a spatter of spilled coffee. His night hadn't exactly been uneventful. The man with him was impeccably dressed, however, and he regarded Hillary with kindly eyes as she entered the room.

"Good morning, Hillary," the chief said, standing. "Hell of a day so far, isn't it?"

"That about sums it up," she said.

"This is Dr. Peter Dworkin. He's with the state medical examiner's office. He's got the autopsy results we've been waiting for."

"Pleased to meet you," the doctor said, rising to extend his hand. "Please sit down, Ms. de Gaetano."

"It must be bad news if you came in person," she commented, sitting slowly and brushing her hair back from her cheek.

"I'm not sure if the news is bad or not," Dr. Dworkin said, sitting and opening a folder. "It is somewhat extraordinary news, however. And since I live in San Francisco, I decided to bring it in person.''

''All right.'' Hillary took a deep breath, steeling herself for whatever he had to say. ''What did you find out?''

''First of all,'' he said, ''your cousin was killed by a single shot fired inside his mouth. I don't think I need to go into details with you about that.''

''No, I found the body.''

''I know. Right then, the wound would be consistent with suicide. In fact, everything about the physical position of the body would say suicide except for the absence of a weapon. But, even without a weapon present, my personal opinion is that it was suicide.''

''Why?'' Her worst fears were coming to life, but Hillary felt more relief than sadness now. Suicide was the only answer that fit what little she knew. The only thing that made any sense at all.

''The angle of the shot,'' the doctor said. ''And the fact that his hands were covered with blood in a pattern consistent with a self-inflicted wound. Nothing had impeded the blood, you understand. Nothing to indicate the presence of another person, that is. And, in the course of our work, we found a mass in your cousin's brain that might very well have brought on suicidal behavior.''

''A mass? What are you talking about?''

''Your cousin had a brain tumor, Ms. de Gaetano. Just behind the frontal lobe.''

''Cancer?''

''Yes, definitely malignant and quite inoperable.''

''It would have killed him?''

''Yes, in a matter of months,'' he said.

''Did he know about the tumor?''

"Not according to his physician. His last physical was over a year ago, and he hadn't complained of any symptoms since then. He wouldn't have felt anything yet, anyway. Nothing that he'd have been suspicious of, that is."

"Meaning what?"

"The position of the tumor and its size was such that it would have placed pressure on areas of the brain governing thought processes and emotions. That's why I suggested that suicidal tendencies were consistent with the tumor."

"You mean that it could be the tumor itself that would make him take his own life? Not knowing that he had brain cancer?"

"Exactly." The doctor nodded his agreement. "It could very easily have produced a manic-depressive state. Elevated emotions one day—extreme happiness, hopefulness and such—and feelings of extreme depression the next."

"Could it have altered his behavior? For instance, might he have taken up gambling to the extreme? Or perhaps made large, unreported donations to charities?"

"Yes, if those things were in his nature to begin with, it might. It would heighten his enjoyment of such things but it wouldn't create an urge to gamble. Was he a gambler before? Friendly card games and such?"

"Yes, Albert was a regular at Friday poker while we were still at it," the chief said. "He never was a good card player, though."

"Well then, the pressure of the tumor may very well have prompted him to go overboard with what was previously a harmless diversion. The same would go for charities, too, if he was a charitable man."

"He was," Hillary said.

"The chief told me that you're having some problems with the IRS," the doctor said. "It would be quite consistent with his condition for him to want to cover up signs of his gambling. You see, the tumor would heighten his embarrassment over his losses and cause him to go to normally illogical extremes to cover them up."

"Even tax evasion?"

"Certainly. And when he'd gone through so much money that he couldn't cover it up anymore, all it would take is an emotional downturn to create the sense of worthlessness that could lead to suicide. Everything he did would feed the feelings that the tumor was already amplifying."

"Bernie said it was suicide," Hillary said softly.

"He did?" Chief McDonald sat forward. "When, last night?"

"Yes," she said. "And Bernie is the one who took the gun from his office."

"He admitted that?"

"He had the gun," she said. "Jeff and I were following him when the storm broke yesterday," she said, hoping to make sense of it all without talk of ghosts. "He said that he took it on impulse because he thought someone was coming into the room. There was no one there, but his fingerprints were on the weapon so he hid it in the old house."

"That would pretty well complete my findings," the doctor said. "All I needed was an explanation for the missing gun."

"But I need a bit more of an explanation than that, I'm afraid," the chief said sternly. "Why do you believe it was suicide when Bernard Foche had the gun?"

"Come now, Chief," she said. "Bernie would never have killed Albert, not when he could make his life miserable instead. You know that. And the fact is that Bernie had papers claiming that Albert owed him a substantial amount of money. Bernie would much rather have held him to the debt than to kill him."

"Maybe, but why were you following Bernie?"

Hillary could see that she wasn't going to get off easily, so she put a weary smile on her face and launched into an explanation of the events leading up to the flood at the old house. It was easy enough to leave her ghost out of it, but it took the better part of an hour to complete the story. When she was finished, the chief was finally satisfied. She was exhausted. All she wanted to do now was to go home to bed.

She did make one stop, however. As tired as she was, she still couldn't help thinking about a dowry, land disputes and a ghost who looked like Jeff Simpson. There had to be an explanation for everything.

Hillary went to *The Napa Press* office to search for her answer and found it staring at her from the wall of Jeff's office. She'd seen the picture of Victor Simpson many times over the years, but it had never been more than a piece of the room's decor. Still, there he was in his dark coat and hat and looking remarkably like his descendant. Once she'd seen the picture, she knew that she was on the right track and attacked the newspaper's files with renewed energy.

She no longer doubted the existence of the ghost of Victor Simpson. Now she sought the information she would need to avert the tragic conclusion that seemed nearly inevitable.

The old papers on file at *The Napa Press* told the story in a rather oblique manner. And they contained

another surprising bit of information. Victor Simpson
had a very specific reason for haunting her. She was a
descendant of his love, Marie de Gaetano, a relative
whom Hillary hadn't even known existed! The story,
as Hillary pieced it together that afternoon, was a tale
of love and betrayal that had come to have far-reaching
consequences.

Victor Simpson, founder of *The Napa Press,* and
Marie de Gaetano had been expected to marry. That
had seemed like a foregone conclusion to everyone
when Victor traveled east in January 1880 to supervise
the purchase and shipping of a new press for the newspaper. But the press wasn't satisfactory, and the time
it took to receive a new one dragged out through the
summer until the fall. By the time he returned, he was
too late for the wedding.

Marie de Gaetano, described in the paper as "a will-
ful beauty," was apparently determined to make her
own decisions, and she eloped with Jerome Foche, the
son of a gambler named André, who had expanded his
poker winnings into a small vineyard up the hill from
the de Gaetano land. It was suspected, quite openly in
Victor's biased reporting of the events, that Jerome
married her as much for the promised dowry of land as
for her beauty. His real motives were lost in time, but
subsequent actions made it clear that old André expected the dowry even though his son had married
Marie without her family's permission. The Foche
family didn't get the land. Marie's father, Alberto,
disowned Marie entirely.

Most of the rest of the story came to Hillary through
several diaries and reporter's notebooks in the book-
case in Jeff's office. Jerome Foche sued for the land
and lost, but Jerome kept his blond beauty at his side

with a jealous eye toward the printer who had prior claim to her heart. It was gossiped that their marriage was far from happy. Rumor had it that she had threatened to leave him many times. Victor didn't report any of that, of course, but it was clear from his diary that he believed it. Whether that was true or not, Jerome was a suspicious and untrusting man who eventually acted on his bitterness and jealousy. Through the evidence of her own haunted dreams, Hillary knew that he acted by striking Victor down and making it look like an accident.

The Napa Press reported Victor's death as a riding accident. His brother, Peter, came out to bury his brother and run the newspaper. Jerome Foche died with his guilty secret in 1922. Marie died eight years later, taking her regrets to her grave. It was not reported whether she ever reconciled with her family.

So the histories of the three families were intertwined in dark and mysterious ways, of which the current generation hadn't any notion. Victor had come back for love and vengeance. He had achieved the latter. But there was no way for him to satisfy his desire for love. Was there any way Hillary could convince the spirit of that fact before he might, in his rage and frustration, cause yet more damage?

It was a matter of life and death for her, and quite possibly Jeff, that she succeed in that task.

EMILY WAS SITTING very quietly behind her desk when Hillary entered the winery office. The woman had only come to work to check on storm damage to the office, intending to return home to finish mopping up her own damp entry porch. She'd arrived only moments before

Hillary, walking in at just the wrong moment for her own peace of mind.

"Emily, what's wrong?" Hillary asked when she saw her. "You're white as a sheet." She hurried to the woman and took her hand. "What happened?"

"I don't know," Emily replied. "I just don't know."

"Goodness, you're trembling." Hillary released her hand with a quick squeeze, rushed to the watercooler and brought back a cup of water. "Drink this."

Emily took the cup and sipped the water, her eyes darting nervously toward the printer on the desk behind where Hillary stood.

"Better?" Hillary crouched beside her, watching some of the spark return to the other woman's gaze.

"Yes, I'm better."

"All right then, what happened?"

"The darnedest thing," Emily said, pausing to get it right in her mind before trying to explain it. "I came in about five minutes ago and the computer was running. That didn't seem altogether strange, so I went to turn it off. But it was off, Hillary."

Hillary glanced back at the computer, a sickening feeling growing within her; she knew the rest of the story.

"Then the printer came on and printed out a sentence," Emily continued. "I guess I stared at it for a while, then I tried to turn it off. Not only was the printer switched off, too, but it gave me a nasty shock when I touched it. Then it printed a couple more sentences and stopped again."

"It did this all by itself?"

"Sure did. Well, I went to unplug the darn thing and got another shock for my troubles. Then an even stranger thing happened. I don't know. Maybe it was just the shock that did it to me.''

"Did what, Emily?"

"I swear I heard someone say, 'Don't touch it.' And it felt like someone pushed me back.'' Emily looked at Hillary as though she expected her to begin laughing. "Like I say, it was probably the shock."

Hillary didn't feel the least bit like laughing. Her heart seemed to have frozen in her chest, the blood stopping still within her. He'd written another poem for her. This was another act of "love," and the last thing she wanted to do was to read that poem.

"Is that all?"

"The printer typed one more sentence. I've been sitting here wondering if maybe I should go have my head examined."

"Don't bother," Hillary said. "The same thing happened to me the other night. I hardly think we're both losing our minds."

"Did you hear a voice?"

"Not right then," she said. She straightened up and tried to put some more spirit into her voice. "Why don't you run home and put your feet up. Everything is fine here."

"Oh, I'll definitely put my feet up," Emily said. "But I've got to see what the page says first."

Hillary would have preferred that she didn't read it, but it couldn't be helped. It would look more suspicious to refuse her that privilege than to allow it. Besides, the words of the poem would most likely seem quite innocuous to someone who didn't know the full story.

Still, it seemed important to Hillary that she read it first, so she walked over and tore the sheet of paper from the printer.

I would my love were near me now,
Beneath our stately tree.
And there to live in lovers' bliss
Through all eternity

The words brought a sudden chill to Hillary's body, and she trembled slightly as she handed the sheet to Emily without a word. A simple love poem, seemingly uncompleted, it didn't look like anything threatening. At least, it didn't seem so to Emily.

"That's it?" She shook her head, smiling now. "I expected some dire threat or something."

"That's it," Hillary said. She shrugged. "You never know what's possible."

"No, I don't suppose you do," Emily said. For a moment, she looked as though she was going to say something else, but she held it back. "I'm going home," she said quickly. "I heard that Jeff was injured. Is that right?"

"Yes," Hillary said. "He's in the hospital, but he'll be just fine."

"Maybe I'll stop in and see him," the older woman replied.

"He'd like that. Take it easy now," Hillary said, putting some animation into her face as she walked with her to the door. "I'm going home to sleep."

"Good. You look like you could use it. Goodbye, dear."

"Goodbye."

Hillary watched her leave without really seeing her go. Once Emily had gone through the door, Hillary's gaze shifted to the window and through to where the old oak tree was hidden behind the rise of land.

There was a feeling of inevitability to the whole thing. In fact, she'd felt that way since leaving the files of *The Napa Press* and coming to the winery. She had expected to find another poem. It was his most logical next move.

The idea of her and Jeff's love seemed to fit all too nicely into the unavoidable nature of it all. Long ago Victor had been denied his love. He'd been killed because of that love. All this time, he'd been waiting to regain what he'd lost. No one but Hillary would have been able to read all of that from those four sparse lines of poetry.

But Hillary knew the meaning of the poem. She knew the purpose behind her visitor's intrusion into her life, the terrible dual purpose that had kept him here until through force of will he was able to complete the task that gave his existence meaning. He'd completed half his task by killing Bernard Foche. And she realized now that all she had to do was to fall asleep. Then he could succeed with the second half of his mission.

Though his motivation might be love, his task could only conclude with her death. And now Hillary felt herself drawn to the hilltop where the dream took place. She had to go if she ever wanted to escape him. She walked out of the winery office and into the bright sunshine that was well on its way toward drying up the remaining signs of the storm. She went willingly, determined to defend herself or die trying.

WITH EMILY'S HELP, Jeff Simpson had managed to retrieve his clothing and leave the hospital. They cut off half of one trouser leg, but the pants were still serviceable for the cause of modesty if not dignity. He left without stopping for the formalities of checking himself out of the hospital and without fully explaining to Emily what had caused him to become so agitated when she'd told him about the incident with the printer.

He'd given the matter a lot of thought since that morning. And since he'd long ago given up doubting the existence of the man, he'd concentrated on figuring out his motives. At first, he couldn't imagine why he would have stood by Hillary as if to taunt Bernard into firing. It seemed at cross purposes with his efforts to help them. He could hardly have wished them harm when only moments later he had helped Jeff get across the burned floor. If his intentions were evil, he would surely have let Jeff fall through.

Still, the thought remained that he had wanted Bernard to fire at Hillary. It was obvious that Bernard had seen him. He was the person to whom Bernie referred when he'd spoken about Albert's death. Bernie had been speaking directly to the ghost then, not to Hillary or Jeff, so he'd definitely seen him.

It had looked so like the ghost was trying to get Hillary killed that Jeff simply couldn't understand it. And then, with a sudden clear knowledge, Jeff knew that there was no other explanation. The ghost *was* trying to kill Hillary. He didn't know everything, but what he did know fit perfectly into place. He had to talk to Hillary. He also realized where he had seen the face before. The ghost looked exactly like the picture of his uncle that hung in his office. The picture had been there for so long that Jeff rarely even noticed it.

When Emily had come to his room instead of Hillary, Jeff's heart sank. And when she told him about the office, he had the dreadful feeling that he was already too late.

THE GROUND BENEATH the ancient oak was perfectly dry, the breeze was as softly reassuring as it had been in the dream, and the man on horseback who approached her had the expectant look of a man who would not be denied anything.

Hillary watched him ride through the vines to the edge of the field with a feeling of déjà vu. She'd seen this before, but from a different perspective. Still, only the changed nature of the field and the sight of the blacktop road with Jeff's car overturned beside it could tell her that she wasn't dreaming now. The dreams, after all, had been so real.

The ghost's love, his all-consuming need, had been real, too.

"It's been so long," he said, stopping about ten feet down the hill, just within the shadow of the huge tree. "I thought I had lost you forever."

"You never had me, Victor," Hillary said, watching him dismount. "I'm not Marie."

"You are," he said. "You are Marie."

"Let me go, Victor."

"No." The man's face twisted with sorrow. He looked at her, and he took two steps closer to her. "I know that I was wrong not to make my feelings more clear from the start, Marie. I should have asked you to wait. I made assumptions about us. I assumed you felt the same as I did."

"I'm not Marie," Hillary insisted, feeling the pain of his loss darkening the air around her as though carried on his words.

"I couldn't have known that I would be back East for so long," he continued, heedless of her interruption. "But you must have gotten my letters. You must have known I would marry no other. Why didn't you wait?"

"Please, Victor," Hillary pleaded. "I don't love you. I'm not Marie."

"I could scarcely believe it when they told me about your marriage. Jerome Foche! That blackguard! How could you have married that posturing fool!"

"I—I couldn't wait." Hillary felt the words being formed by her lips and heard her voice speak them, but they weren't the words she had meant to say. "I was a fool, Victor," she said, panic rising in her throat as she did.

"No, Marie. It wasn't you." Victor came closer now, holding his hand out to her. Hillary drew back. "I should have asked you before I left. I should have gone to your father and made my intentions clear to everyone. It is all my misdeed."

"Hush, my darling. You could hardly have expected me to be lured by Jerome's fancy words," she said. Hillary let the words come out, feeling herself in the grip of a power beyond her comprehension. "I wanted to spite you, and I wanted to spite my family. I did both, I'm afraid, and I paid for it."

"As did I," Victor said. "Your darling husband waylaid me on the road. I didn't fall from my horse, Marie, I was struck down."

"No, you can't mean that," Hillary said, feeling almost as though Marie were speaking. "You've had your revenge for that," she said, now feeling that she was clearly doing her own talking. "You've killed an innocent man for revenge."

"Innocent? The man forged papers to blackmail Albert de Gaetano," Victor said angrily. "He falsified tax records and called to report the errors in the accounts. He was not innocent."

"But he wasn't a murderer."

"Yes he was! He saw Albert's weakness and introduced him to people who could exploit it. He knew full well what he was doing when he engineered the poor man's debts! It was only a matter of time before an honorable man would have no choice but to end his life, and he knew it."

"No. He couldn't have known that," she said. Behind Victor, Emily Pragger's car pulled to a stop on the shoulder of the road and Jeff got out and began limping through the vines toward them. "You murdered an innocent man," Hillary said again, hoping to keep Victor from seeing Jeff.

"No one in that family has been innocent since Jerome murdered me," he insisted. "I won't waste any more talk on the matter. Come now, Marie. I've waited too long."

Once more the feeling of his love and the pain he felt in his separation from his loved one flooded over her. The man was so lonely. All these years alone with only the thought of his lost love to sustain him...it was such a waste.

She knew now that the dream of the two of them together on the hilltop had truly been a dream. It was his century-old dream of their reunion, not a fact of history replayed in her sleeping mind. The dream of the murder had been true. The embracing lovers had been nothing more than his heartfelt desire, and it saddened her to think that he had never married his true love. And he would never have that now.

"Come, Marie," he repeated.

"I'm not Marie," she said, feeling dizzy now, her legs barely able to sustain her.

"Yes you are!" he said. With two quick strides he grasped her hand. "Come with me now," he said.

"You can't have her!" Jeff reached the top of the hill, winded from the effort of the climb. "You don't have anyone handy to kill her for you here. I doubt that you could bring yourself to do it personally."

"Get back!" The ghost released Hillary and turned toward Jeff. "I won't let you stop me."

Hillary felt too weak to do anything but watch the two men for the moment.

"And I won't let you take her," Jeff said, standing defiantly in front of the apparition.

"Don't get in my way!"

"Or what? You'll kill me?" Jeff moved toward him, stepping between him and Hillary. "If you'd wanted me dead, you would have killed me already. I'm your flesh and blood, Victor. You can't harm me any more than you could harm her."

"You don't know what I can do," Victor said, though he seemed less sure now. "I'll do what I must to release Marie."

"You missed your chance already," Jeff said. He stooped beside Hillary, who looked up at the man in black in pity.

"You planned the whole thing, didn't you?" she asked. "You got me back here because you knew that Albert needed help. But when Albert killed himself you saw the perfect opportunity, didn't you? You made

Bernie take the gun, made him hide it in the house, even made him hold off on saying anything to me about the loan so that we would suspect him. And you burned our files to make sure we wouldn't find out about Albert too quickly."

"And it worked, too," Victor said.

"You were going to get Bernie to kill Hillary by making him think he was shooting you," Jeff said then. "And then you would be free to get revenge."

"I have my revenge," he replied. "Now I must have my love."

"She's my love," Jeff said, holding Hillary firmly in his arms. "Are you so bitter that you'll take away my happiness just when I have it within reach? Are you that selfish? If you are, then you'd better kill me, too, because I don't want to live without her!"

"She is my Marie!"

"No she's not!" Jeff held Hillary tightly.

Hillary felt suddenly so tired, so awfully tired. She found herself wishing that she could just sleep and let fate take its course. But then, very quietly in the back of her mind, she thought she heard a voice saying, "No, you will not lose your love as I lost mine. You will not sleep. You will not make the same mistake that I made."

"Wait," Hillary said, but that was all she could get out before a tingling sensation washed over her and she fell back securely in Jeff's loving embrace.

Victor stepped back, a look of awed joy growing on his tortured features. He was staring past Jeff and Hillary. All three of them watched, open-mouthed.

A woman was there, dressed in the gingham dress she'd worn in Hillary's dream. She became as seemingly substantial as Victor was, her smile radiating love just as his voice had.

"Marie," he said, taking her into his arms.

"Victor."

Their kiss seemed to create a glow in the air beneath the venerable oak, and the soft light grew to flood over them with a feeling of peace incorporated into the light. Hillary felt her fatigue slipping away as the glow warmed her. And when the light receded, the two long-separated lovers were gone.

"I love you," Jeff said softly.

They embraced beneath the lovers' oak, their kisses every bit as ardent and eternal as the reunion kiss they'd just witnessed. And they were every bit as inseparable as the two who had gone before.

Epilogue

"The sins of the fathers are visited on the sons," Hillary said quietly.

Outside the solarium, the sun was sinking behind the mountains and bathing Hillary and Jeff in ruby light as they sat snuggled together on the rattan couch. Words couldn't express the happiness they felt in each other's arms; neither could they fully encompass the sense of loss with which their recent experiences had acquainted them.

The de Gaetano family Bible that Hillary was holding in her lap as they watched the sunset contained a list of every child born in their new American home. Births and deaths were faithfully recorded right up until the present, when the family dwindled steadily down to the last name: Hillary de Gaetano.

The only blight on the rows of carefully lettered names and dates occurred near the top. A thick scribbling covered one name in the list as though someone had decided that one of the children listed hadn't existed, after all. When Hillary held the page up to the light and looked very carefully, however, she could still make out the name, Marie de Gaetano.

But such was her love of her family that she'd remained with them in spirit just as Victor remained tied to the earth by his love of his lost Marie. Old love, eternal love, their love could not rest until it had achieved the union they'd been denied.

"I never thought to look for a reason behind everything," Jeff said, pausing to kiss the top of Hillary's head, which rested on his shoulder. "I just assumed the Foches were congenitally ornery."

"I wonder if Bernie knew why it began," Hillary said. "I don't suppose it matters. He learned to distrust people from his father, who learned it from his."

"They had paid for Victor's murder years ago, really. All of that bad feeling over the years had most likely grown from guilt over the crime."

"It's easy to hate someone who makes you feel guilty," she said.

"Now, if Victor had trusted the company to ship his press out without supervision, he would have lived a long and happy life," Jeff said.

"And we'd be blood relatives," she reminded him. "Don't get too wistful."

"No, I guess I don't mind the way it all worked out."

"Have you heard from Mr. Chambers?"

"Yes, he's recovering nicely," Jeff said. "If James Winger had left Lemuel alone we probably wouldn't have been able to connect him to Bernard's little scheme at all."

"No," she agreed. "There was nothing on paper, and it would have been Lemuel's word against his about the phone call. He didn't strike me as the nervous type when we met him."

"No, but he was certainly greedy. He wanted to get into the wine business on the cheap." Jeff laughed. "And how is the wine business these days?"

"Better. We won't be in the clear until we convince the IRS that there was no criminal intent," she said, snuggling closer. "But I can't seem to work up much worry about that just at the moment."

"That medical examiner can help there. I think it will all work out. Have you figured out how far in the hole you are?"

"The books are a mess," she said. "But we'll survive. I think Albert gave more to charity than he ever lost gambling."

"That's a novel way to go broke," Jeff commented with a wry laugh. "Donating yourself into the poorhouse."

"Poor Albert."

They sat in silence for a moment, the last rays of the sun fading away as they watched. Overhead, the stars glimmered like diamonds sewn into the fabric of Heaven.

"I'll love you forever," Jeff said quietly.

"I know," Hillary replied, turning to accept his kiss. "I think I've always known that. I love you, Jeff."

"People always knew there was going to be a marriage between the Simpsons and the de Gaetanos," he said. "I don't suppose they expected it to take an extra hundred years."

"Oh, well," Hillary said with a sigh. "Better late than never." Hillary felt in her heart that there were two other lovers out there somewhere who agreed with her completely. Two others, like them, who loved forever.

ROMANCE IS A YEARLONG EVENT!

Celebrate the most romantic day of the year with MY VALENTINE! (February)

CRYSTAL CREEK
When you come for a visit Texas-style, you won't want to leave! (March)

Celebrate the joy, excitement and adjustment that comes with being JUST MARRIED! (April)

Go back in time and discover the West as it was meant to be . . . UNTAMED— Maverick Hearts! (July)

LINGERING SHADOWS
New York Times bestselling author Penny Jordan brings you her latest blockbuster. Don't miss it! (August)

BACK BY POPULAR DEMAND!!!
Calloway Corners, involving stories of four sisters coping with family, business and romance! (September)

FRIENDS, FAMILIES, LOVERS
Join us for these heartwarming love stories that evoke memories of family and friends. (October)

Capture the magic and romance of Christmas past with HARLEQUIN HISTORICAL CHRISTMAS STORIES! (November)

WATCH FOR FURTHER DETAILS IN ALL HARLEQUIN BOOKS!

CALEND